MAY 16, 2005

Mark,

To a good friend, And
A great brother!

Thanks,

Chris

LAST EFFECTS

Christopher Joyce

First edition © Christopher Joyce

Library of Congress Catalog Number: 2004097291
ISBN: 0-9762214-0-3 (hard cover)

Cover design and layout
Carolyn Stonehouse

CENTENNIAL BOOKS

1591 Chapel Hill Drive, Alexandria, VA 22304

Printed in the United States of America

In memory of Robert "Bobby" Leahy, PFC, 3rd Battalion, 9th Marines, killed in action June, 1968 in Quang Tri Province, Vietnam.

"For many are called, but few are chosen." *Matthew 22:14*

PROLOGUE

The empty warehouses were World War II vintage Quonset huts, abandoned for a decade, unsuitable for any purpose. Combined assaults from annual monsoons, insect generations, creeping foliage, human neglect, and the passage of time took their cumulative toll. Slated demolition would hasten their gradual slide into collapse.

Master Sergeant Harry Bouchard and his demolition contractor took a final walk-through. "Make sure you put construction fencing around the site," he cautioned. "I don't want some kid sneaking onto the base and getting into trouble. I don't need any more problems with the locals."

"Will do, Top. By the way, what were these buildings used for?"

"All sorts of stuff," the sergeant replied. "When they were first built, they were barracks. My first tour out here was in 1966, and by then we used them to stow gear for guys heading south."

"South? Not sure I follow."

"That's shorthand for Vietnam. Marines going to war stopped in Okinawa, stowed their stateside gear, got their shots and jungle fatigues and shipped out. They picked their stuff up when they rotated home, assuming they weren't med-evacs—or something worse."

The hard hat grunted his thanks. "I'll get my guys started on the demolition tomorrow. After we put a fence up," he added.

They found the duffel bag the next day. Collapsing the second building, they discovered it lodged between the corrugated steel shell and short concrete anchoring wall. Had it been empty, the crew would have tossed it in with the rest of the demolition debris. But it wasn't—its contents filled out the fabric cylinder, secured by a combination lock at its top. The faded name stenciled in black was still discernible: *D. P. Keane.*

The contractor put the sea bag in the bed of his pickup. Later that afternoon, satisfied the demolition site was secure, he swung by the base property office. Hefting the sea bag to his shoulder, he went inside the single story building and up to the desk where Sergeant Bouchard was enjoying his end-of-the-day cup of coffee. He rotated the bag to the floor in front of the desk.

"Looks like this guy Keane never came back to collect his duffle bag, Top. Wonder if he was one of your med-evacs, or worse?"

CHAPTER ONE

Jack Keane put the finishing touches to the invoice for his final month's work at Compugraph. They had agreed a flat monthly fee at the start of the engagement, four months back. It had been a good tour, and he would miss the people and the work—and the fees.

The assignment was straightforward. Step in as Compugraph's interim CEO, fill in during the search for a permanent successor. *Permanent was a bit of an exaggeration,* Jack reminded himself. In fact, top executive life spans were getting shorter, and the demand for a competent pair of hands to oversee things during periods of executive suite vacancy was steadily increasing.

In the big picture sense, Jack Keane didn't believe that the shortening tenure of corporate top leadership was a good thing. Developing a firm grasp of what makes a business tick takes time, and you need a firm grounding in a company's operations to have any chance of taking it to a higher level. But in the micro-economic sense, the appetite for fast turnover in the executive tier, the willingness to "throw the bum out, get a new horse to ride," was a tonic for his business. Jack Keane, doing business as Impact Consulting, had never been so busy.

Compugraph's last CEO went through the JK (for Jack Keane) four-phase leadership life cycle at warp speed. Jack's inner voice branded these phases with Motown song titles he deemed descriptive: Phase one was "Love Child," when the new guy or girl (most were guys) is recruited with the expectation that he or she will wave a magic leadership wand and heal all that ails the enterprise at once. You know the situation has ripened to phase two, "Try a Little Tenderness," when people start going on about how the new guy just needs more time to find his voice. "Sitting on the Dock of the Bay," phase three, is when all parties realize things are still stuck in a groove nobody likes; somehow the problems have not been miraculously healed, but we're not sure exactly what to do. The terminal phase four, "Shotgun," is where we "shoot him on the run, now." Cycle times *were* speeding up.

Fourteen weeks earlier, Keane recommended to his investor clients that they jettison the incumbent CEO immediately. The advice wasn't whimsical or self-serving. The fastest way for Jack to destroy his business was to shoot from the hip when dispensing advice, especially regarding top leadership. He first invested a week at Compugraph "obtaining an understanding," the label he used with clients for the start-up period. His private label was "kicking the tires," but that pedestrian terminology, though accurate, didn't suit his four-thousand-dollars a day billing rate.

He had no personal grudge or animosity for the incumbent CEO. He seemed like a nice fellow, and Keane guessed he was loved at home and in the community. Like Hollywood's depiction of Mafia chieftains talking among themselves, it was strictly business. Unlike those movie dramatics, however, no one from Compugraph was going for a ride to the Jersey Meadowlands for terminal disposition. In Jack's experience, jettisoned CEOs ended up driving off in company provided cars, well insulated by the cash bursting from their pockets—or purses.

No, Jack framed the recommendation to Compugraph's owners through the lens of efficiency. What is the CEO's primary role? "Leaders lead," JK management maxim #1. Since Mr. Compugraph CEO was not leading and wasn't going to improve with time or coaching, the only question left was the timing of his exit.

The second question Jack answered that first week was, "Is he doing more harm than good?" Were the owners better off leaving him in place while they found a suitable replacement? Or should they cut their losses right then? Jack invoked management maxim #8: "Never aim to wound."

That approach could be called aggressive, even ruthless. Not surprisingly, Jack didn't think so. He believed it was efficient and equitable, directly relating compensation received to what the quality gurus called "worth what paid for." The CEO's high octane compensation—$400K base salary, performance bonus of almost fifty percent of base, *plus* long term incentives—bore no relation to his impact. At some point, the imbalance had to be resolved. The only remaining question was timing.

Compugraph's private owners initially desired to keep Mr. UB (pronounced *Hughbee*, Jack's generic nickname for miscast senior executives) on board until they found a replacement, but Jack disabused them of that notion. "You're better off without him. He's doing more harm than good. Bite the bullet, cash him out, and launch the search for a successor." They accepted Jack's advice with the proviso that Keane join as interim CEO while they looked for a replacement.

LAST EFFECTS

Mr. UB (shorthand for *UnaBomber, destroyer of shareholder value*) thanked Jack for getting the owners to act. In their final meeting, UB said he sensed that "things were not a hundred percent with the board." *I rest my case*, Jack thought.

The final invoice completed, Jack hit Send, turned away from the flat panel display, and looked out at the traffic on Route 7. "Let's wrap this up for tonight, mate," he said for his own benefit.

As he pulled onto the Interstate 495 ramp heading east, Jack's cell phone chirped.

"Jack, it's Ephraim. Can you talk?" Ephraim Halperin was Jack's favorite combination CPA and attorney. He packaged the best qualities of each—sharp, methodical, disciplined, principled, determined—with only traces of the less desirable features of either. He knew what he knew, didn't nickel and dime you on his hours, and most important, the professional competences came in a good business sense wrapper.

"I can talk. What's up?"

"Jack, I had another call from Roland Haskins today. He asked me if you could lend a hand on a problem they have. Firm's called Quantamica. Roland and the other investors were blind-sided with an unexpected cash call. They need a quick assessment of what's going on, and he's intent on parachuting you in to get a handle on things."

"What's the company name again?"

"Quantamica. Their long suit is software—pattern recognition applications."

"Who comes up with those names, Ephraim? Sounds like a resort in Mexico," Jack injected gratuitously. *Get back on point*, he chastised himself. "What do you think is going on?"

"Not enough data to compute, Jack, but it smells. Cash burn a lot faster than anyone expected. CFO says he's as surprised as everyone else they need more cash so soon. Top team looks a bit inbred, too. I guess I'm not sure if it's simply stupidity or something worse."

Jack considered. "Well, let's do this. Why don't you, Roland and I get together for breakfast next week, hear what he has to say, and go from there?"

"Okay. I'll call Roland and get it set up."

Jack reflected (or *noodled*, in his inner vernacular) how quickly a welcome hiatus between assignments was evaporating. It hadn't always been that way. When he first set up shop, he had one client in hand and an aspiration to be self-employed and solvent. That was eight years ago. Since then, he had built a strong reputation as a high impact business consultant with a small but growing following.

The best testimonial to his impact was the volume of repeat business. More than half his clients knew his work personally from prior assignments. Part of his value was flexibility, like jumping in immediately for a client like Roland Haskins. Impact Consulting generated over $500,000 in client billings the year before, plus Jack received private equity in lieu of cash on two engagements. And the current year's pace of business was chugging along fine, thank you.

Jack took the Interstate 395 North exit off the Beltway, heading for Washington D.C. He owned a condominium in Alexandria, just south of Old Town. Typically, he'd stay on the Beltway to the Route 1 exit, but that night he decided to drop in on his father.

David Keane lived in a senior facility, also in Alexandria. As Jack exited I-395 at Duke Street, following his at least weekly route to his dad, he reflected on how much things had changed from his childhood.

The senior Keane had been a career civil servant with the federal government. After graduating from high school in 1939, David Keane was drafted into the army right before the start of WWII and served in the Signal Corps. He met Jack's mother, Ruth Gordon, while he was hospitalized with appendicitis, soon after his discharge in 1945. She was a registered nurse who did her training in New York and migrated to Washington during the war. Theirs was a "bond that began with a bedpan," as she described it.

Jack's brother, Daniel, was born in 1948 and for five years was the only child. Jack was born in 1953. Daniel was the trailblazer of the family—strong athlete, good student, paper-boy, Eagle Scout, and the consummate older brother to Jack.

Daniel graduated from high school in 1966 and enlisted in the Marines. Jack recalled his brother's rationale. "Jack, no offense to Dad and his army service, but if you have to fight, wouldn't you get the best training so you have the greatest chance of survival? And wouldn't you rather depend on other guys who were volunteers too?" Jack replayed that logic to his father at the dinner table one night when Daniel was not there. His father shook his head, smiled, and said, "Daniel has his own mind."

Daniel shipped out to Vietnam in 1967 and died in January, 1968. The circumstances of his older brother's death were murky to Jack. He knew his brother did not die in combat. He recalled the family saying that Daniel's death was "a tragedy, a real waste." Whenever Jack raised the subject, David Keane's response ran along similar lines. "Your brother's death was a metaphor for that mess in Vietnam. He went into the lion's den, but he didn't come out."

After Daniel's death, Jack Keane turned inward. He was a successful, though unchallenged, student. He devoted his after school hours and summer energies to work, first a paper route, then clerking in the local five-and-dime, and finally stock boy at the local supermarket. He supplemented those jobs with landscaping and clean-up spots in the neighborhood. It wasn't solely money that drove him to work. He enjoyed the independence money gave him, but the distinct identity he derived from work was more compelling. He was good at it, took on added responsibility quickly, and liked being recognized as capable and committed. He maintained that focus as he grew up. Competence and commitment were Impact Consulting's brand attributes. He believed all work had dignity, and was adamant that every job added to his personal capital stock. When asked how long he had been a professional, his honest response was, "Since I was ten."

Jack graduated from the University of Virginia in 1975 with a degree in Economics. After three years with a major corporation, he earned a graduate degree from the Darden School in 1980. He joined the consulting practice of one of the big accounting firms, rising rapidly to partner.

Ruth Keane died of cancer in 1983. Her husband never fully recovered from her death. He progressed from the family home in Alexandria to an in-town apartment and finally to a senior citizen facility, all in a decade.

As he parked in front of the Birchmere, Jack recalled that his parents died a lot in 1968 when Daniel didn't come back from Vietnam.

CHAPTER TWO

It was after 9:00 P.M. when Jack finally got home from visiting his father. *This isn't going to be easy,* he thought, *so let's just get it done.*

The duffle bag his father presented to him earlier that evening sat in the middle of Jack's living room floor, its faded green canvas contrasting with the wheat-toned carpet. He walked to the kitchen, grabbed a tumbler, half filled it with crushed ice, then three fingers of Johnny Walker Black Label. In the living room, he sat in the more worn of two flame patterned armchairs and studied the bag.

If Daniel were here, Jack reflected, *he'd correct me.* "It's not a duffle bag, Jack. We call it a sea bag." Home on his first Marine Corps leave, Daniel introduced Jack to a new lexicon. Jack's memory gushed recollections of conversation from that first and final visit home. "We have different names for a lot of things, Jack. It's not a bed, it's a rack; a stairway is a ladder; it's not your head, it's your gourd," the last delivered with that short barking laugh that came so easily to Daniel. The tape in Jack's mind played on. "The M-14 rifle is an air cooled, gas operated, magazine fed, semi-automatic infantry weapon that fires the 7.62 millimeter NATO round." He recalled his brother's skin head—"whitewalls" according to him—as they sat down to dinner the first night of Daniel's leave and the excitement, energy, and seeming invulnerability that emanated from his older brother.

Jack turned from his memories of Daniel in 1967 to the sea bag before him. He recalled it in their Alexandria home more than thirty years before, sitting in the hallway by the front door as Jack came in from school. Its olive drab color was sharper then as it stood rigidly to attention. After a moment, Jack noticed the black-stenciled name and number on its side and realized his big brother was home on leave! Later that evening Jack passed the sea bag again on his way upstairs to bed. He recalled a flash of jealousy. He saw the sea bag then as a challenge to their brotherly bond, an interloper. Daniel and the bag had already seen things that were foreign to Jack, and soon they'd be off together again.

And now there it was again, as if transported forward suddenly through a time portal. He felt a twinge of that old jealousy as he stared at the aged, faded, bent traveler.

■　　■　　■　　■

Earlier that evening at the Birchmere, Jack knew immediately that something was wrong. Evelyn, the LPN on the three-to-eleven shift, avoided his glance and didn't acknowledge his greeting. Jack assumed his father was at the root of her cool response; that David Keane, Room 14, was having one of his infrequent but challenging ornery spells.

The door to his father's studio apartment was closed, unusual at that time of night. David Keane normally kept his door open throughout the day and early evening. "It's hospitable, and I'm running for mayor," he said in his typical jocular mood. He had recently started closing the door when he went to bed though. He told Jack three weeks earlier that he awoke and discovered Mildred, his dementia-suffering neighbor, sitting on his bed in the middle of the night. "Do you want some company?" she asked. After that, David Keane closed his door when he got into bed.

Jack knocked and, hearing no response, went in. David Keane was sitting on the bed, facing the windows. The blinds were drawn. He sat staring forward and did not acknowledge Jack's presence.

"Dad, it's me," Jack announced. "How are you doing?"

David Keane took a moment to register that Jack was there and speaking to him. "Okay, son," he volunteered, still not turning. "I'm okay. Just feeling wrung out tonight, like... oh, just real tired."

"Have they been treating you okay, Dad? Are you eating?"

"Oh, all that's fine. No, I've been thinking about Daniel all afternoon, and I just feel completely spent." He still did not make eye contact, but in profile Jack could make out the dark half circle under his father's right eye.

"Dad, I know there's been a lot of that quagmire stuff on the news lately, with all sorts of Vietnam comparisons, but I hope you're not letting that eat at you?"

It was as if Jack slapped his father. David Keane turned and faced him squarely, the anger setting in his face. "It's not the news that got me thinking, Jack. It's that." He pointed to the closet.

"That?" Jack followed his dad's finger but saw nothing. He walked to the closet, pulled back the louvered door and peered inside. His father's wash-and-wear shirts, which he liked to launder himself, hung in their usual place. Slacks, also permanent press, were to the right of the shirts. Bending a bit at the knee, Jack saw it, propped against the back wall of the closet. A duffel bag.

"It came at lunchtime," David Keane said. "They brought it in, told me it had just been found. They wanted to return it to the family, very sorry and all that. Finally, they asked me where I wanted it. I just pointed to the closet. I didn't know what to say. Since then I've been sitting here thinking. My boy Daniel, my oldest. I forgot how I miss him."

Jack expected tears, but instead his father went quiet, rocking back and forth gently on the side of the bed. Jack stared at him a while, finally sat next to him and put an arm around his shoulders.

"I'll be okay, Jack. You're a good son. I love you. I want to go to bed now, okay?"

"Are you sure, Dad?" Jack offered to stay the night. "They can put a cot in here. I think I better stay."

"No, son, you go home. And take that with you." He nodded at the closet. "I don't want to see it again."

Jack hefted the sea bag to his shoulder, just as Daniel had done more than thirty years before.

"I'm just glad your mother isn't alive to feel the pain again."

Jack stopped by the nursing station on his way out and asked Evelyn to keep an eye on his dad. David Keane had had a difficult day.

■　　■　　■　　■

Now the sea bag's contents lay spread across Jack's living room carpet, sorted into piles as the bag disgorged its innards. Military uniforms were in one stack; a pair of military boots started a second; civilian clothes in another; one pair of shoes—his brother's "cockroach stompers," so called because of their pointy toes—keeping the boots company; a pair of madras bathing trunks with the civilian clothes; a black silky jacket with *Vietnam* and a dragon in yellow embroidery on its back.

Finally, at the bottom of the bag, Jack hit paper. First, a photo album; then a rubber band bound stack of letters and postcards; next, two paperback books, Harold Robbins' *The Adventurers* and a Nero Wolfe mystery. Further down, he retrieved his brother's *Guidebook for Marines* and on the next dive, a deck of Bicycle playing cards. Finally, fingertips trolling the coarse surface of the bottom panel, he came up with a leather wallet.

Jack upended the sea bag and shook it to be sure it was empty. Only then did he realize it smelled of mildew and took a strong pull on the Scotch to allay the odor. Methodically, he put each pile into plastic or paper bags. He'd decide what to do with them later.

He sat down heavily in his reading chair, pulled on the Scotch again, and picked up the photo album. Its soft green cover was accurately but needlessly emblazoned *Photo Album* in cheap gold lettering. A dozen two-sided, peel up plastic covered pages. Inside the cover in Daniel's neat printing, *Daniel Keane, USMC*. Penciled in further down the page were two dates, *March 15, June 4,* followed by *Mouchie, Rick L., pals forever* in the same hand.

On the title page was a cut-out photo of Daniel in his Marine jungle fatigues. Underneath was inscribed *Memoirs of a Running Dog of American Imperialism*. That was Daniel's sense of humor, Jack reflected, co-opting enemy propaganda for the title of his memory album.

Jack studied the photo closely. He had never seen it before. It captured his brother's spirit. It was spontaneous, not posed. The cameraman caught his subject in the doorway of a hut, maybe startled him by shouting his name, and captured a surprised look. Jack recalled seeing a matinee with his brother years before, a Western. The Indian chief protested when his picture was taken, believing the photograph captured his spirit—and he wanted it back. The picture before Jack captured Daniel's youthful exuberance.

Jack rested his eyes a few minutes. He stretched his legs and settled further into the padded armchair that was his reading, thinking and TV viewing receptacle. When he awoke, it was past midnight. The album lay on his lap, still open to the picture of Daniel.

Jack closed the album and said goodnight to his brother.

CHAPTER THREE

They had scheduled a 9:00 A.M. breakfast meeting at the Tower Club in Tysons Corner. Jack was always at least ten minutes early for an appointment and got there at 8:45. He skimmed the front page of *The Wall Street Journal* and waited for Ephraim and Roland Haskins.

Jack kept predicting that the business "scandal of the week" atmosphere of the last two years would dissipate and let business reporting return to less sensational fare. So far, that forecast was wide of the mark. On page one above the fold the Journal highlighted another earnings restatement by a Fortune 500 company. The *What's News* column recounted the sacking of senior leadership, closing with the boilerplate corporate pronouncement expressing "regrets, but by our actions, we hope to put this episode behind us." Jack invoked JK management maxim #9, "You're not a pig until you start squealing."

He heard the elevator doors open and picked up the tattoo of footsteps, then conversation, as Ephraim and Roland rounded the corner briskly, heading for the seventeenth floor lounge where Jack waited.

"Good morning, Roland," Jack said and nodded a greeting to Ephraim.

"Hey, Jack," Roland replied. "Thanks for meeting on short notice."

They presented themselves to the hostess who led them to a vacant table, already set for three, an island in a sea of occupied tables. "Let's have something more private," Roland told the hostess. They settled in at a table at the less populated far end of the room.

"Okay if we order the buffet?" Roland suggested. "That'll give us more time undisturbed." While water, juice, and coffee were delivered, the three grazed along the buffet line. Jack took his usual breakfast: Raisin Bran, skim milk, a banana. He was first back to the table, waiting until both men returned.

Haskins launched into the Quantamica situation while applying a uniform veneer of butter to a toasted English muffin. Ephraim worked quietly on his fruit plate, attention focused on Roland.

"We got involved with Quantamica fifteen months back, when we were approached about taking a stake in the company." *We* meant Rock Creek Capital, the investment group he chaired. "Quantamica was part of the Kimball Group, but they didn't see it as core to their business and decided to cash out. They approached us and, after what we thought was a good look, we took the lead in the carve out."

Jack was about to ask how much Rock Creek paid but decided to let Roland tell the story his way. The investor stabbed sharply at the yoke of his over-easy egg. Jack suspected he was about to get an answer.

"The investor group put up $40 million in cash, plus the new company issued $20 million in high yield debt. Our view was we could earn a thirty per cent return simply by cutting out the flab they had developed under Kimball and build a more focused stand-alone business. We planned on flipping it in three to five years."

Haskins described major events since their investment: the unexpected departure of the CEO soon after the spin out; the prolonged process to find a replacement; the vacuum at the top during the hiatus, which triggered additional executive departures. Jack listened while his brain kibitzed: *How many times have we seen this movie? At least ten variations.* The acquisition consummated with aggressive aspirations, initial churn at the top, resetting expectations, strolls along the Rue de la Regret—it was all déja vu.

Roland approached current events. "So now we have the latest call from the CFO, that Quantamica has just about burnt through its cash reserves and needs to access its bank credit line. That's purely a stopgap, and he's forecasting they'll need another ten million from the investor group. Tapping the credit line can carry them a while, but I need someone to go in and lift the hood, tell us whether we should hang tough with those guys or just hang them."

Roland looked at Ephraim, then turned to Jack. "I understand you're available. I need you to put some time in there, give us your assessment. What do you say?"

Jack had anticipated the question and his response since he awoke that morning. The balance sheet was in his frontal lobe, composed as he went through his morning routine and during the drive out to Tysons. On the asset side, *yes* meant additional work, cash flow for the next month and maybe beyond, and possible referrals downstream. Among the liabilities he included seeing the same business movie again and something new—concern about David Keane's health and need for Jack's assistance. Like a footnote disclosure in a mental balance sheet, the sudden arrival of the wayward sea bag triggered unknown impacts for his father. *And also for me,* he admitted.

"Roland, I appreciate your offer. I'd like to lend a hand. I think the timing could work, but there's one thing. My dad had a nasty surprise yesterday and I'm concerned about his health."

"Was that after we spoke?" Ephraim asked.

Jack nodded and went on with his answer. "I need time to assess how much support my father needs, and I don't want to over-commit to you and then under-deliver."

"Is he in the hospital, Jack?"

"No, it wasn't a medical surprise, Ephraim. He had some very disturbing news yesterday. And I'm not sure how he'll react."

"Sorry to hear about your father, Jack," Roland offered. "Let's do this. Assess the situation on the home front, and let's talk in a few days. We'll decide then how to proceed."

▪   ▪   ▪   ▪

Jack swung into the Birchmere parking lot just before 11:00 A.M. He and Ephraim had stayed at the table another half-hour, discussing Quantamica and David Keane. Ephraim was aware Jack had an older brother who was long dead but had never heard the circumstances. As Jack told about the arrival of the sea bag he was reminded how little he knew about his brother's tour in Vietnam and how he died. The final year of Daniel's life, his whole overseas experience, was a thin chapter filed under *Fog of War* in Jack's memory.

He recalled in detail, however, the aftershocks his brother's death caused in January, 1968. Coming in from his after school job, he discovered his parents seated in the living room, not normal at that time of day. Ruth Keane's red eyes, hunched shoulders, David's consoling arm wrapped around her and the taught lines of his father's face all telegraphed something significant. David Keane had risen from the sofa and enveloped Jack in his arms. "Son, your brother is gone." Jack stared over his father's shoulder at his mother, not knowing what to say, realizing there was nothing to say. Daniel was gone. He had been away for a year, and now he was gone for good. The family and each of them individually would walk a different path from that moment forward, a path without a son named Daniel for Ruth and David, a world without their first-born; for Jack, an empty space where his older brother had stood for fifteen years. Jack recalled lying on his bed that night and thinking a fault had opened in time and space and his brother had dropped through it. "Where are you, Daniel?" he asked before he fell asleep.

He did not press his father for details at first. When he asked how Daniel died, David Keane's explanation was frugal. "It was an accident, Jack, a silly damn accident." When Jack pushed for detail, David offered a bit more. "He was in a war zone. There are plenty of casualties that aren't caused by enemy fire. That's just the nature of war. Your brother's death was an accident." When the matter came up again a few days later, David Keane added, "Accidents happen, especially when a bunch of nineteen-year-olds are walking around with loaded rifles. It stinks, but it doesn't change the outcome. Daniel is dead. And right now, we have to focus on getting your mother through this."

And they came through it, but not intact. The triangle that resulted from Daniel's death was radically different in shape, texture, and stability from the four-legged Keane family stool prior to January, 1968. Jack started assembling the matrix in his mind, the before and after descriptors of the family—from energetic to passive, optimistic to . . . He broke that line of thought and turned to the immediate problem of his father.

David Keane was sleeping when Jack got to the room, so he settled quietly into the corner armchair, listening to his father's rhythmic breathing. After fifteen minutes, he headed down the hallway to the nursing station. The duty LPN's nametag read Gertrude, a new face. He introduced himself and asked about David Keane's routine last night and that morning.

"Nothing extraordinary this morning, and the night nurse didn't pass on anything special," she replied, looking at David Keane's chart. "What's he doing now?"

"Sleeping."

"Is that usual for your father at midday?"

"I don't think so, Gertrude, but I'm no expert on his late morning routine."

"His chart indicates he was awake at 2:00 A.M. Sounds like he had a restless night."

Jack decided to leave. "Well, please let him know I was here when he wakes up, okay?"

"Won't need to," the nurse replied, her eyes focused over Jack's shoulder. "Looks like Mr. Keane has already seen you." Turning, he saw his father walking toward him, steadying himself with the hand rail.

After a hug, they ambled back to David's room. Jack sat on the edge of the bed, while David Keane lowered himself slowly into the armchair where Jack sat earlier. "How are you doing, Dad?"

"I'm fine, Son. Feeling a bit slow today, but I was up pretty late."

"Gertrude said you were awake at two this morning. When did you get to sleep?"

"Not sure what time it was. Went to bed around eleven, tossed and turned for thirty minutes, so I got up again. I remember reading that if you don't go to sleep in fifteen minutes, get up and do something. It's a problem I don't often have." David Keane prided himself on being able to sleep anywhere, even wrapped in a poncho in an inch of water, one of his army stories.

"I thought a lot about that duffel bag, Jack. Funny how it shows up now, thirty years late. The major said something about Okinawa and a storage area they were tearing down. I vaguely remember Daniel writing me something about Okinawa, but why the bag was there is a mystery to me."

"What major, Dad?"

"This major," the elder Keane replied, handing Jack a card he pulled from his shirt pocket—the same wash and wear shirt he wore the day before. Jack made a mental note to come back to personal hygiene later. The card read, *Major Ralph Gutierrez, Headquarters Company, Marine Barracks, Washington, D.C.,* with a phone contact.

"He's the one who delivered the bag," David Keane continued. "I told you that yesterday. He stayed a while, didn't have much information. I asked how they found me? Said he stopped by the house, and the new owners told him I lived here." David Keane sold the family house in the Del Ray section of Alexandria to a young couple ten years before. They stayed in touch with the old man, albeit infrequently. Jack wondered what would have happened to the sea bag if the house had turned over again.

"Dad, did this Major Gutierrez say anything else?"

"He said it was Daniel's gear; some clothing, personal effects, some of his uniforms; stuff like that. Said they inspected it when they sent it back from Okinawa. Have you been through it yet, Jack?"

"I started last night, but I haven't finished."

"Well, Son, you decide what to do with the contents. I have everything I need of Daniel's."

Jack stayed for lunch, glad to see his father had an appetite.

28

CHAPTER FOUR

Jack just made the 4:10 P.M. flight from San Francisco International to Washington Dulles. He had finished his initial kick-the-tires visit to Quantamica's headquarters in the San Francisco Bay area, an interesting two days. He spent the first day with the CEO, CFO, and a number of other senior executives. While they didn't roll out the welcome carpet, they understood his presence was prerequisite to their continued access to Rock Creek's cash. Day two was diving deeper in relevant areas: reviewing recent sales, talking to software developers, probing Quantamica's recent forecasts. Liberal doses of walking around, asking questions, getting different answers depending on who he talked to, and developing a sense of the climate supplemented his focus on the concrete.

Settled into his first-class seat, Jack made a mental note to call Quantamica Asia Pacific's managing director in Hong Kong early the next week. You couldn't miss the apparent sales success in that region—double-digit quarter-to-quarter growth the last three quarters—and he wanted to hear first hand from the senior person on the ground just what was driving it. He also needed to understand why their top line success had not yet translated into cash collections for Quantamica's local affiliate.

Once the Boeing 777 reached altitude, Jack knocked out a trip summary for his client, then picked at the penne pasta that looked like the best meal choice. Eventually he reached for Daniel's photo album, brought almost as an afterthought, as he sipped his coffee.

Memoirs was an eclectic collection. Beyond the title page, which sported the full length picture of Daniel, were six additional pages of photos and other mementos. The rest of the album was empty, space Daniel never got to fill. Paper money samples took up the second page—a Vietnamese ten piaster note with a boy atop a water buffalo, followed by a ten dollar Military Payment Certificate, which Jack assumed was script used by Americans in the combat theater. The plastic covering the currency samples had yellowed with time, but the certificates appeared intact.

On the facing page, a series of photos captured scenes along a highway, apparently in Vietnam. The uppermost shot, in color, looked like a shrine or temple with bright banners streaming from its arches, emblazoned with inscriptions Jack assumed were Vietnamese. The rest of the page was a mix of village and highway scenes—peasants, motorbikes, pedicabs, bicycles, minibuses, all angled down toward their subjects—taken perhaps from the back of a flatbed truck. The last photo on the page at bottom right was Daniel standing with a young Vietnamese woman in front a large building Jack assumed was a warehouse.

On the next page, everything was black and white, scenes on a military base—warehouses, Quonset huts, tents, some with heavy equipment in the background, one that looked like a mess hall or club. Each photo captured an individual or small group of Marines, the surrounding area as backdrop, never the subject. Jack's attention was drawn to mid-page, Daniel standing in the entrance to a sandbagged bunker, rifle in right hand, smiling up at the photographer.

The pictures on the following page were beach scenes. Some of the men wore fatigues, some shorts; two photos captured young Marines and two Caucasian women — *Nurses?* Jack wondered — the ocean in the background; another centered on a volleyball game. Jack found his older brother in only one, posed with another grinning Marine, each raising a can of beer in half toast toward the lens.

A plastic encased certificate greeted Jack's eye as he flipped the page. The familiar Marine Corps anchor and globe was embossed at the top, announcing to all present that Lance Corporal Daniel P. Keane had successfully completed the Non-Commissioned Officer School at Camp Butler, Okinawa, in November, 1967. Facing it on the following page, another official document stated that Lance Corporal Keane was promoted to corporal, effective October, 1967, signed by a Colonel F. W. Martin, USMC. So his brother had left Vietnam for a short spell in Okinawa, Jack realized, attending the NCO school after his elevation to corporal.

On the following page, Daniel had saved a copy of a letter he had written.

Date: 1 Nov 1967

To: Colonel F. W. Martin

Re: Request for Transfer to Combined Action Platoon

Sir:

I have been selected to attend the Non-Commissioned Officer School in Okinawa for the next three weeks. After completion of this training, I respectfully

LAST EFFECTS

request a transfer to the Combined Action Platoon program here in I Corps. I have completed over half my thirteen month tour of duty in-country, and would appreciate the opportunity to serve in a more direct capacity for the remainder of my assignment.

I appreciate any consideration you can give this request.

Respectfully,

Daniel Keane
Corporal, USMC

Jack flipped back a page to the promotion certificate. The same Colonel Martin appeared there too. Daniel's certificate of promotion to corporal was printed on heavy paper, almost cardboard. The plastic overcoat had lost most of its adhesiveness, and the certificate was no longer centered on the album page. Jack picked delicately at the corner of the cover, intent on re-centering the document, but it separated from the page. *Damn*, Jack thought, as he caught the paper's edge, but it was too late. He had it in his hand.

His fingertips felt something else. Turning the certificate over, Jack discovered a single folded sheet of notepaper taped to the back. He didn't want to risk damaging it, but curiosity trumped caution, and he peeled the tape up carefully. He unfolded the paper and read.

Note for the record
I spoke to Gunny Walters before I left Red Beach and let him know that I am not going to join the team. He was not happy,

32

but told me he would square things with the boys in the band. Told me to go off to Okinawa to NCO School. He'll use the three weeks I'm gone to patch things up, so that I could get along OK. As a favor, he asked me to carry a package here. I don't know what was in it. While I'm gone, he says he'll lubricate the transfer process with the C.O. so that I get out of Red Beach ASAP. Will support my request for the CAP assignment. Says I'll probably get my ass shot off, but if that's what I want, it's OK with him.

Just in case things don't go right, I'm leaving this note.

Daniel Keane
10 November 1967

Jack stared at the thirty-five-year old note, penned in his brother's mixture of block letters and cursive. What team did Daniel Keane not join? Why the need to get out of Red Beach? What did he carry back to Okinawa as a favor to Gunny Walters?

He looked out the window of the 777, making its final approach to Dulles in pouring rain. It was a perfect metaphor for the storm gathering in his mind.

CHAPTER FIVE

Major Gutierrez suggested Baja Fresh for their lunch meeting when Jack called him earlier that morning. "The food's fresh. I start early, so if it works for you, let's target for eleven-thirty, okay?"

Jack's weekend had flashed by with a Saturday morning jog, some puttering around his condominium, then on to a bachelor's chores: pick up/drop off at the dry cleaners, food shopping, car wash, preventive maintenance around the house. Saturday night was a formal dinner party in Georgetown, a stag event for him. He was home in bed, alone, by midnight.

Sunday was relaxing. He spent time with his father after breakfast, then bicycled north along the Potomac to Carterrock and back.

He didn't prefer the monastic life, but he didn't fight it, either. Jack Keane had married twice, had a number of relationships in between, but adapted to the solitary life after his second wife, Susan, died three years before. They had no children, were close, and Jack was not optimistic about marrying again, at least he was not yet motivated to go out and try.

He spent Monday morning at the Tysons office, then headed into the District on I-66. He parked and walked the two blocks to the restaurant at the corner of 19th and K Streets. Major Gutierrez was easy to recognize in his tan uniform, *tropicals* as Daniel called them. After introductions, they ordered and took a table fronting K Street.

Jack offered to pay, but the major declined. "But I appreciate the offer, Mr. Keane."

"It's Jack, major. Mr. Keane's my father."

By mutual but unspoken assent, they focused on the food. Ralph Gutierrez ate deliberately, working clockwise through the chicken burrito, guacamole, salsa, and chips. Jack noted he wasn't a finger licker.

"I'm sorry to reopen an old wound," Gutierrez offered as he pushed his plate to the side. "I could argue we should have just lost that sea bag again and not stir things up, but that's not the way we do things. How's your father?"

"He's all right, I think. I was concerned right after your visit, but he seems more settled now."

"Well, I'm glad to hear that, and for what it's worth, I'm sorry for any pain we caused your dad... and you."

Jack wasn't sure how to introduce the trigger for his call that morning. On the telephone, he said he had some clarifying questions he hoped to get answers to. He did not divulge his discovery of Daniel's hidden note.

"How long have you been in the Marine Corps, Major Gutierrez?"

"It's Ralph. Coming up on forty years," he smiled.

"Does this happen often?" Jack asked, searching for a path to bring up Daniel's note.

"*This* being the return of personal effects to next of kin thirty years late?" Without waiting for an answer, Gutierrez went on. "I've never heard of it before, but my guess is it has happened a few times. North of three million troops rotated through WesPac, Jack. Sorry—WesPac is military speak for Western Pacific, shorthand for Vietnam in most cases. I have to believe we managed to lose more that one guy's gear in that time." He paused. "But here, the guy was your brother, and he didn't come home."

"Do you know how it was found? Where was it?"

Ralph related a shorthand version of events as he understood them, including the role Okinawa played for Marines heading to Vietnam. "Most of the men going in after 1966 were replacements. They'd stop in Okinawa, leave behind stateside stuff, get shots, and two or three days later land in Da Nang. From there, they'd get assigned to a unit."

"What do you know about my brother?"

"Not a lot. I went through the sea bag, which is SOP before we return anything to family. Don't want something embarrassing turning up, if you know what I mean. I checked his service record, know that he was with a unit called Force Logistics Command, a corporal, good service record, enlisted out of high school, and that he died in early 1968."

"Can you tell me how he died? The circumstances?"

Gutierrez didn't answer immediately. "Jack, your brother's record indicates he didn't die in combat. A fuller explanation should have been provided to your father at the time. Typically, that would be face to face, from an officer or senior non-com. The details provided then are your best source. What did your father tell you?"

"Not a lot—that it was an accident in a war zone, and a lot of deaths aren't combat related. Then the conversation tails off, and I've never pushed him for more details. We hadn't discussed it for years," Jack said.

"Well, for what it's worth, that's all too true. About ten per cent of our casualties in Vietnam were not from combat. I recall one of my squad falling off the front of our

Amtrak on a routine patrol, crushed underneath the treads, not a mark on him. So I know from personal experience about non-combat related casualties."

"So you were in Vietnam?"

"Yes, after your brother."

"I didn't realize officers led squads. I thought they commanded platoons, or companies?"

"I wasn't an officer then, Jack. I was a NCO, like your brother. I made officer later. I'm what's called a mustang, promoted from the ranks."

Jack stared down at the table, thinking, then came to a decision. Reaching into his pocket, he unfolded a photocopy of Daniel's note. "What do you make of this?" He pushed it across the table.

Gutierrez skimmed the note, looked at Jack, then reread it slowly.

"Where'd that come from?"

"The sea bag. It was taped to the back of a document in his photo album."

Ralph's eyes drifted back to the paper. He studied it another minute, then handed it back to Jack.

"What do you make of it, Ralph? What's he talking about?"

"Hard to tell, Jack. Reads like your brother was not a happy camper. Appears he told this Gunnery Sergeant Walters, and they were working a transfer. Not clear what 'joining the team' means . . . " Ralph let the sentence drift to a close, as if undecided how to complete it.

"But what about the package that he delivered for Walters? What's that all about?"

"Impossible to say." Realizing he sounded abrupt, Gutierrez added, "Listen, it could be any of a number of things. Maybe someone was shipping home a load of hash, maybe a .45 caliber pistol, or whatever."

"I need to find out why Daniel wrote that. It's clear he was in a bad situation. He talks about things not going right. Reads like he was being pressured into something that he didn't want to be part of, doesn't it?"

Gutierrez returned Jack's stare, finally responding. "Mind if we walk a few blocks?"

They headed south on 19th Street, moving briskly through the lunchtime sidewalk traffic. Jack followed the major's lead as they reached Pennsylvania Avenue, then headed east. At the corner of 17th, they turned south.

They walked another five minutes in silence. At the base of the Washington Monument, Ralph veered off the path for one of the park benches. Jack sat beside him, and both watched the pedestrian traffic circling the monument.

The Marine's eye caught the stand of American flags snapping in the breeze. "I love the Marine Corps, Jack. I've had a great career. It's changed some in forty years, but the fundamentals, the basic values, are constant. During Vietnam the Corps expanded beyond its capacity. We lost some effectiveness, our edge during Vietnam, because we grew too fast. Discipline suffered, part because of too many recruits and not enough experienced non-coms, part from the failure to connect the war to national interest. Drugs hurt also, though that's overblown. We also failed to maintain unit cohesiveness. The whole replacement approach, sending in individuals versus intact units, was flawed, and caused a lot of our problems."

Jack realized he was hearing an analysis Ralph had developed over time and presented before. "I say this because the Marine Corps your brother served with in 1967 *was* different. As I look back, it has a surreal quality. We talk about the fog of war today almost as much as we say 'in harm's way.' But I'd say that Vietnam is better described as 'the forever war.' It went on and on with no resolution." Ralph paused to choose his next words.

"I suspect what your brother carried to Okinawa was drugs, but that's just a guess. It may have been harmless. My point being, whatever it was, that was over thirty years ago. I doubt you can get an answer to your question, but what if you do? It won't change the outcome. So my advice, Jack, is to let it go. File it with the other unanswered questions about your brother. Take comfort that the final piece of him has now come home."

CHAPTER SIX

At five-thirty Tuesday morning, Jack was on a conference call with Alex Chung, Quantamica Asia Pacific's managing director in Hong Kong, to discuss the affiliate's strong sales performance. He spent the first ten minutes listening politely as Chung waxed on about the strength of Quantamica's software compared to the competition. "The software sells itself, Mr. Keane. My salesmen are just order takers, to tell the truth. We have the strongest products in the region."

After a few more minutes of Alex's local color commentary, Jack turned the conversation to cash, specifically the build-up in client receivables. "Why aren't we paid faster, Alex? You've got six months worth of sales that you haven't turned into cash yet. How come?"

Chung pointed to two causes. "We are victims of our own success, Mr. Keane. The build-up in unpaid invoices is because we have grown so quickly." Chung paused for a moment, apparently waiting for Jack to congratulate him. Hearing nothing, he continued. "And we have the challenge of local business practice." That came with a sigh, as if Chung apologized for his Asian colleagues. "Asian companies pay slower than American customers, Mr. Keane. We will be paid eventually. They pay slow, but they always pay."

After discussing their customer list, Jack asked for details on who had not paid, then added, "And send me your current sales pipeline. I want to see the new business prospect list."

"We will get right on it, Mr. Keane. You'll see, everything is fine. They just pay slower than American customers."

Jack was skeptical despite the assurances. His bullshit detector had registered *moderate* during his visit to the U.S. company's headquarters the week before. The needle just went up a notch to amber: *caution*. The senior team at Quantamica had to grow top line sales, to scale the business up for an initial public offering down the road. *Methinks they may be too clever by half*, Jack thought, but he needed more data. He'd take a look at the backup information and go from there.

He had processed his discussion with Ralph Gutierrez continuously for the past eighteen hours. He replayed Daniel's note, the meeting with Gutierrez, David Keane's reticence, the errant sea bag—a collage of memories, current events, and extrapolations all quietly percolating.

Coming upstairs after a work out to cool off before showering, he sat at the computer screen in his home office. He keyed *Vietnam casualties* into the search engine and got back 103,000 possibilities. Scrolling through the first few pages, nothing looked helpful, but on page four he found a database managed by National Archives. He populated the requested data fields with what he knew:

Military Service?	*USMC*
Country of Casualty?	*South Vietnam*
Type of Casualty?	Jack left it blank.

41

LAST EFFECTS

Name?	*Keane, Daniel P.*
Date of Death?	*After 1 Jan 1968*
Home State Code?	*VA*

He took another swallow of coffee while the engine searched. In a few moments, one record popped on his screen.

Keane, Daniel P.; Service Number 2206677; Date of Death January 8, 1968; Force Logistics Command, Da Nang; Cause of Death, Q.

What does Q mean? He scrolled backward, looking for an explanation. Clicking on *Type of Casualty,* there were twenty-three different codes and meanings displayed. Skimming down the alphabetized list, he located code Q, third from last.

Q meant suicide.

That explained things in a new way—his father's reticence, the truncated and private grieving, the lack of military pomp at Daniel's funeral. In that cold January of 1968, he had linked his family's compartmentalization of grief directly to the way Daniel died. Not hostile action, simply back luck; not force of arms, but an accident. At the time, that explained his parent's insistence on a family-only service.

The new datum, the coded value that spelled self-destruction, corrupted the logic and pattern to Daniel's life. While the Keanes weren't outwardly religious, they believed in the sanctity of life. Jack recalled a boyhood incident that crystallized that for him. A neighbor suffering from depression had closed herself and the family station wagon in the garage. The V-8 was still running when they found her. The Keanes agreed that only a complete mental collapse could explain that.

Jack tried to imagine Daniel taking his own life. Could things get so bad, so depressed, that suicide was the preferred option? Had his brother become a dead-ender? Jack rejected that out of hand. It just didn't fit. It wasn't Daniel.

His inner voice pushed back. *What do you know about it, Jack? You've never been in the military.* Maybe Daniel started using drugs. Perhaps that girl in the picture . . . Jack interrupted the thought: *No way!* Daniel surely had vices, but the idea that he had a drug dependency, or any dependency like that, was a non-starter.

And there was the hidden note, tucked away in Okinawa. Why did Daniel write it, plus take the added precaution of secreting it in his album? If it was a CYA note only, meant to shield him from some future charge, why not just leave it with his gear?

No, Daniel didn't take his own life. Jack didn't buy that. But what did happen? Was it a coding error, some clerk sloppily keying in Q instead of T or R, converting *Accidental Homicide* or *Accidental Self-Destruction* to *Suicide*? Or was the coding correct but the explanation offered at the time flawed?

Of the twenty-three available codes, there was none for intentional homicide—murder.

■   ■   ■   ■

The Judge Advocate General's office was close to Gutierrez's location at Marine Barracks. He covered the distance to the Washington Navy Yard at a route step, arriving at 9:00 A.M. Ralph had called a close associate, Marine Major Ed Stanley, immediately after the lunchtime meeting the day before, and his legal rabbi suggested they share a cup of Stanley's "wicked brew" in the morning.

LAST EFFECTS

Daniel Keane's note shook Gutierrez. He went to lunch assuming Keane knew his brother had taken his own life. But as their conversation progressed, he realized Jack was in the dark. Apparently, the elder Keane had not been candid with his son—and others?—about the cause of death.

That gave Ralph his first surprise in the conversation, and he opted to respect the father's dissimulation. Jack could learn the facts easily, but so far had honored his father's ruse. Gutierrez didn't see himself as the agent of full disclosure, supplementing what the father had already communicated to his son. He had no idea of the context at that time, or further specifics that may have been provided to David Keane. Q could have many meanings under the umbrella of suicide.

The private note was the second curve ball in their dialogue. If "disclosure" could be brushed aside as family business, the new revelation could not. Corporal Keane's word choice was dramatic. Ralph hypothesized that Daniel was caught up in some nasty business in Da Nang. God knows there was enough going on, between cheap and plentiful drugs, kickbacks, highways built to nowhere at taxpayer expense. Much was exposed during and immediately after the war, Ralph recalled, a number of officers and non-coms charged with fraud, secret bank accounts, the whole nine yards.

Perhaps Corporal Keane, hag ridden by some of the muck he was wrestling in, had too much to drink one night, decided he was a worthless piece of whatever, and took the quick way out. Ralph had personally seen bursts of temporary insanity in the nexus of alcohol, drugs, fatigue, depression, fear—a toxic brew. A war zone provided quick and terminal remedies—rifles, grenades, detonation cord, even something more exotic, if you were into special effects.

But then, Keane was a bit of an enigma. Ralph reviewed his one page service summary. Enlisted out of high school; clean record up to the point of his death; made rank quickly; no discipline problems. And then there was the corporal's letter to his C.O., requesting transfer to the CAP program. Ralph read it as he went through the kid's effects. Gutierrez knew that was not light duty. Combined Action units were small, village based Marine and Vietnamese teams, forging a closer bond with the locals in their operating area. Because of their small size, they were juicy targets. Many were overrun during Tet 1968.

The note took on additional import with Keane's explosive verbiage, his reference to the "boys in the band." Ralph wondered if there was a homosexual angle, given that interesting label, but then dismissed the notion. His Marine Corps certainly had all points of the sexual orientation compass represented, but the idea of a self-contained cluster? That was unlikely, given that men were assigned, not self selected, to units.

"Morning, short-timer," Ed Stanley greeted him, as he came down the hall from the JAG commander's office. "Walk with me."

Ralph followed to the small kitchen abutting the hallway, where each got a mug of black coffee. Back at Stanley's office, Gutierrez took one of the two hard-backed, unpadded chairs facing the lawyer's desk. Looking around, he took in the unkempt office, a sharp contrast to Stanley's brain.

"How many weeks to go, or is it days?" Ed pushed back in his chair and lifted his feet to the right corner of the desk.

"Yes," Ralph answered. Gutierrez was due to formally retire in two months, but with accumulated leave, he'd depart Marine Barracks at the end of the week. After savoring the attorney's momentary confusion, he continued.

"Depends how you count, counsel. Sixty days to the official event. Four days and I clear my desk."

"So what's the plan, man? Marry some rich widow and help her maintain a lavish and decadent lifestyle? Start a competitor for the History Channel called *Mail Call 2*, hosted by your friend and mine, Major Ralph Gutierrez? Or return as a K Street commando, fronting for these capitalist swine defense contractors?" Ed delivered the diatribe in a rising voice, the final words echoing down the hallway.

"Might want to tone it down," Ralph smiled. "Otherwise, you'll be joining me in the retirement line sooner than planned." As if on cue, Ed's commanding officer put his head through the door. Both men got to their feet.

"As you were, gentlemen," he said. "Just wanted to say hello to your guest." Colonel Mike Carpenter and Ralph shook hands. "Why are you meeting with an ACLU wannabe, Ralph? You haven't done something naughty?"

"No, sir. Just need some informal coaching on how to handle a thirty-year-old problem."

"Sounds complicated. I'll get out while the getting's good." At the door the colonel turned and nodded to Major Stanley. "And yes, major, I did catch the quip about capitalist swine. Might tone down that rhetoric a bit, as your guest suggested. Something a bit less inflammatory, like" — Carpenter feigned searching for a word — "defense pork? See you at your retirement party, major."

Both men were smiling as they sat back down, Ed assuming his commander meant Ralph's retirement. "So what's the scoop, Ralph? What's the dangling issue from Vietnam?"

He used the next ten minutes to review the case of the wayward sea bag. The JAG officer took notes, asking no questions. When Ralph finished, he took both mugs to the kitchen for a refill, giving the counselor a few minutes to absorb things.

When he returned, Stanley was thumbing through a JAG case summary at his bookcase. Ralph noted 1968-73 on the binding. "Have I tripped a wire, Ed? Related to an old case?"

"Not that I know of. Just wanted to get a sense of some of the courts martial activity back in prehistoric times. Well before my time, you know."

Ed sat across from him again, referring to his notes. "Did you keep a copy of Corporal Keane's note?"

"No."

"Think the brother will give you one?"

"Don't see why not. I can ask."

"Do that. How'd you leave things with the brother?" Ed looked up from his note pad.

"I recommended he let it go. Said there was probably no way of discovering the truth."

"Think he'll follow your advice?"

"I doubt it. Strikes me as a guy who needs to know *why*. Appears to be a high powered consultant. I took a peek at his website after we met. Reads like quiet but forceful competence."

"Do you have his card?"

"I'll leave a copy."

"Okay, so what's your question?" Ed laid the pencil down on the pad.

"What else do I need to do?"

"You mean legally? Morally? Philosophically?"

"Let's start with legally."

"Not a thing. First, you have no knowledge that a crime has been committed, that there's been any violation of the Uniform Code of Military Justice. Next, you returned the personal effects to next of kin and went a step beyond in meeting the brother. He shared information he represents came from the brother's effects, which may or may not have UCMJ implications. Third, not sharing the official classification of Corporal Keane's death with the brother was a judgment call, and I concur with that judgment. Best left to the father to communicate with his remaining son as he sees fit."

"Okay, let's hit the other non-legal responsibilities," Gutierrez said. "What's your advice?"

"Not my department, amigo. Suggest you visit the chaplain. However, as a friend, I'll offer random observations, not to be confused with legal advice. Agreed?"

"Yes to the caveat. No to visiting the chaplain."

Stanley smiled. "Okay. Get a copy of the brother's note, write a cover memo to Criminal Investigations Division, single page, relating how you obtained it, and hand that off. I see no further value you can add, given the nature of the issue and the rapid expiration of your own active duty clock."

"What's CID going to do?"

"My guess is they'll file it. They've got their hands full with current cases, given your everyday, mundane criminality that comes with human nature," Ed replied. "But that's not your department, is it, short-timer?"

"I suppose not. Thank you, counsel." Ralph rose from the chair, shook his friend's hand, and headed for the door.

"Oh, one more gratuitous thought on post-retirement occupations. Promise me you are not going to write your book. We have enough books in the world!"

"I promise."

CHAPTER SEVEN

Jack took the rest of Tuesday as a mental health day. No client calls, no e-mails, just personal reflection time. The discovery of his brother's purported suicide was a body blow, similar to when Susan died in a traffic accident on the George Washington Parkway. But as he reflected, his rejection of the institutional answer hardened: Daniel did not kill himself. Something else happened.

But his parents had accepted the bureaucratic explanation. What did David Keane know about Daniel, about the circumstances of his death, that he had not told Jack? Was the shame of the suicide label enough to make his father suppress any doubt he had at the time? Jack knew he couldn't put himself in his father's shoes, feel what he felt— the impacts he balanced for himself, his family, and his dead son's memory.

And something else occurred. Jack had been a willing partner in the family conspiracy of silence. What he conveniently labeled "sparing Dad's feelings" harbored a measure of self-interest. *He* preferred to leave things alone, too. Jack once read that ninety per cent of communication is non-verbal. He knew all along his father was saying more than, "It's too painful for me." Telegraphed non-verbally, "It's too painful for you, too."

The time had come, triggered by the arrival of the package from the past, to set things right. But how? He needed to confront the untruth between them, not David Keane. Better to approach things with his father the way Jack's mind was processing them. Share Daniel's note, discuss the questions it raised, enlist his father in the search for the truth.

Still he hesitated. Daniel may have been caught up in something dishonorable. Should he expose his father to additional pain? And himself?

Jack weighed the possible secondary impacts—on reputation, on memories, on relationships—in his analytic way. He was convinced the potential for truth outweighed the risk in further discovery. Taking a copy of Daniel's note, he headed to the Birchmere.

He arrived after dinner, heading to his father's apartment. The door open, he picked up the strains of *Don Giovanni* as he got closer. David Keane sat in the solitary armchair, eyes closed, apparently lost in the opera. As Jack entered, the eyes opened and he started to pull himself up from the chair.

"Don't get up, Dad." As they shook hands, David settled back into the chair. He lowered the volume with the remote.

"Have you had dinner?" Jack asked.

"Oh yes. It's Tuesday, spaghetti and meatballs. The pasta's too fat. I guess the cook never heard of number nine. Funny, how the thickness changes the taste." Jack had heard that critique before, one of the filler comments his dad used more often as the years progressed.

After some talk about the weather, politics, issues in the Church (David Keane being Catholic), Jack said he had finished unpacking the sea bag. "That's fine, Son. You do whatever is best with Daniel's things. Like I said, I don't want or need any of it. By the way, how's your business doing?"

"Fine, Dad, but I need to talk about Daniel. I found a note with his things." He handed it to his father.

David Keane took the outstretched paper, his eyes focused on his son. "Is this something I need to read, Jack?"

He didn't reply. With a sigh, the old man unfolded the note, took his glasses from his shirt pocket, and read. Finished, he stared at the paper. "What do you make of this, Jack?"

"I don't know what to make of it, Dad, just like what to make of Daniel's supposed suicide."

David's eyes snapped up to his son's. "Where did you get that?"

"I finally did some research of my own. I didn't want to badger you with questions, so I took a look for what I could find."

"So much for a family's right to privacy," David Keane protested. "Now it's public information?"

"It's not that easy, Dad. I went looking for it, plus I know the particulars. I was surprised, but after a while, it explains a lot."

"What the hell does it explain? I haven't come up with a good explanation in thirty-five years, and now you've broken the code in a few days?" David Keane took deep breaths, calming himself. After a moment, he continued. "Jack, there is no explanation. There never was. Your brother had everything to live for, and then he goes and throws it all away? And for what? To get high on some pills or other crap, and then self-destruct during some psychedelic trip?" He paused again for deep breathing, wrestling for control.

"They told me he probably had a drug problem. It wasn't uncommon, especially in rear areas—easy access, ready supply, boredom. But it never made sense, just like that war." The last was delivered as tears rolled down the deep seams of the elder Keane's face. He took off his glasses, wiped his eyes with a handkerchief.

Jack stood over his father and put his hands on his shoulders. Not a hug, more laying on hands. "Dad, I'm sorry to bring it all back. I agree. It doesn't make sense. I don't believe Daniel took his own life. I think he's telling us that. Something was wrong; more than the war, more than with him. Something fundamental, maybe criminal, that he was caught up in. And it's all wrapped up in his death."

David Keane pushed himself up to face his son. "What are you saying? Your brother was killed? Why? By who?"

"That's what I mean to find out."

CHAPTER EIGHT

Eric Walters finished his fresh squeezed Florida orange juice, drinking in the panoramic view of the Atlantic from his patio. *Life is good*, he thought, especially when you have the shekels to live well. It was a style of living he had grown accustomed to, radically at odds with his humble roots.

Top Walters retired from the Corps after twenty years with half pay and full benefits. Soon after, he emigrated to Jacksonville Beach, Florida. Within a year, he purchased the Surfside Motel, on the strip between Route A1A and the beach. It was a bargain. Jacksonville Beach had fallen on hard times, with the scale back in military budgets after Vietnam, the aging ocean front properties, and the city's lack of a beautification plan and budget. The prior owner had a soft spot for retired military, given his own service and the special place the armed forces occupied in Jacksonville. With three major installations, the military was the city's biggest employer. All that contributed to a sweet deal for the retired master sergeant.

Walters bought two adjoining parcels at reasonable prices in the next five years, all settled with cash. The individual transactions were low profile, just the way Top Walters wanted. No questions arose about the retired Marine's access to cash, and enough time had passed to blur memories of the circumstances of his arrival in 1978.

The Surfside and surrounding properties met the wrecking ball in 1990, and a high-end, oceanfront condominium complex, Ocean Dunes, covered the land Eric assembled so patiently over twelve years. He reserved the penthouse with its uninhibited view of the Atlantic rollers for himself.

Life is good, he repeated.

CHAPTER NINE

The sailboat slipped out into the Potomac at 8:15 A.M. The breeze, strong sun, and clear weather forecast promised a beautiful day on the river. Ralph Gutierrez had sailed "a bit" as he described it, and contributed strong if not fully able hands to work the thirty-five-foot boat.

Hands On had been in Jack's hands for five years. Berthed at the marina immediately south of Reagan National Airport, Jack tried to take her out every weekend in season. Client commitments permitting, he supplemented his weekend avocation with the occasional weekday sail.

That day's objective, however, was not about the joy of sailing. He had reached a conclusion, and the sail was to implement it. To start his quest for the truth, Jack needed a plan to focus his efforts and a guide to navigate unfamiliar terrain.

■   ■   ■   ■

He telephoned Gutierrez the day before, catching the major at his Barracks extension. Anticipating resistance to a second meeting, he was prepared to exert a full court press.

After initial pleasantries, Jack moved to his purpose. "Ralph, I'd like to get together again." He waited for the push back, and Gutierrez did not disappoint him.

"Jack, I'm not sure there's anything left to discuss. I don't see how I can help any more."

"I agree. You've done everything you can. I want to discuss options. Call it a trusted advisor request. I need guidance and direction." Hearing no immediate rebuttal, he suggested a sail together. Nothing too rigorous, just morning coffee on the Potomac.

Gutierrez chastised himself for not letting the call flow through to voice mail. He didn't relish the thought of being trapped on a boat in the Potomac, revisiting the case of Corporal Keane. How to blow the guy off politely, he wondered?

"Jack, I appreciate the invite, but I'm down to short strokes, and I need to tie up loose ends to get out of here on schedule." Ralph had an empty In tray and the lightest duty of his career, and the lie sounded like one.

"My brother didn't get out on schedule, major."

Ralph didn't have a comeback. After a thirty second pause, he acquiesced. They agreed to meet one last time, at the marina at eight.

■　　　■　　　■　　　■

Out in the river with sailing space, Jack brewed coffee. They sat in the cockpit, Jack steering, *Hands On* making slow progress south toward Mount Vernon. Their conversation had been focused and monosyllabic while getting underway.

"Thanks for meeting again, Ralph," Jack began. "I realize it's above and beyond."

"Jack, I'm here because of your brother. It was sincere when I said I had nothing else to offer. You said you need some guidance. Well, I'm here to listen, and I've got an hour."

"Are you close to retirement, Ralph? Or are you targeting for a half century?"

Ralph laughed, the unexpected question and his reaction easing the tension somewhat. He told Jack his retirement date, but he'd wrap up his current assignment the end of the week. Then he'd start a seven week leave.

"Any immediate plans? Or will you kick back for a while?"

The guy is direct, Gutierrez thought. *That's refreshing.* "I don't mind you asking, Jack," Ralph responded, giving Jack permission to enter his personal space after the fact. "No immediate plans. For the first time in my adult life, there're no orders to my next assignment. Initially, I'll go with the flow. Why do you ask?"

"Have you thought about consulting, setting up as an independent contractor?"

"Not much. Frankly, I'm not interested in being a retread."

"Retread?" The term was new to Jack.

"Meaning out of uniform but still serving the military. A door opener, facilitator, client relations type, pitching work back to the people I've spent my career with. Not that they're bad to work with. It's about me, my desire for something different."

Jack tacked to port, both men instinctively tucking their heads as the boom passed above them. "Guess that rules out going to the Gulf as a security consultant, huh? Too much like what you've done before?"

"A bit. It's come up, but that's for younger guys."

"Ralph, do you remember the movie *The Magnificent Seven?*"

Now where are we going with that? Ralph wondered. He turned back towards the Virginia shoreline, considering. It wasn't too far to swim, he humored himself.

"Yes, Jack. Why?"

"You recall the bandit chief telling the good guys to 'ride on'? That's how I heard your advice about trying to get to the truth of Daniel's death. *Ride on.* Well, I can't."

"Okay, Jack, then don't. I think you're setting yourself up for failure, but you're a big boy. But what's that got to do with me?"

"I need help. For at least a month, maybe two."

Ralph, not responding, continued to study the Virginia shore passing on his right.

"Someone who knows their way around the Marines, around Vietnam. Somebody available, who I can work with. You meet two of those, and my hope is that the third . . . well, I'm asking if you'll work with me."

Ralph turned to face Jack. "So much for my advice to let it go."

Hands On made steady progress in silence for the next hundred yards. Both men kept their own counsel, Jack focused on the boat, Ralph on the shore.

Jack broke the silence. "You suggested I let it go because the pain and frustration outweigh a truth I'm unlikely to discover, right? That's what I heard."

"True, though I'd phrase it differently. I don't believe the truth is discoverable. And I see more pain, for you and your dad."

Jack considered. After checking lines, the clearance ahead, glances through all points of the compass, he turned to Ralph. "I appreciate that, Ralph. But I came to a different conclusion, probably because I weigh the risks different. Fundamentally, I don't accept my brother killed himself. It's an oxymoron—Daniel and suicide. That's not how he died." Jack spoke with quiet emphasis.

"Then his sea bag suddenly appears. That's not random. There's a reason. My brother penned that note because something was wrong, and I mean to find out what it was." Another pause as Jack focused on the boat.

"Final point. My dad told me the Marine body escort in 1968 implied my brother was doing drugs. I put a low probability on that; not zero, but low. So I can't connect the dots, Ralph, with the official explanation of suicide."

Ralph considered Jack's points while accepting a coffee refill. He enjoyed the boat's forward motion, the sense of slow but steady progress. The presentation was stronger than the fact base supporting it. He presented arguments forcefully and cogently, but the strength of Jack's delivery hadn't changed Ralph's mind. He still believed the truth was beyond reach. Too many years, too few facts, and the fogging of memory that mirrored the fading photos in the brother's album. Many of the actors in the drama must be dead. It was a stretch they'd locate anyone who knew or accurately remembered Corporal Daniel Keane, much less the circumstances of his death.

But Ralph sympathized with Jack's need to know and belief that events have a purpose. After years of leading men, sometimes in battle, always in preparation, he also believed things happen for a reason.

"What did you have in mind?"

Jack proposed a weekly retainer of $10,000, with a four week minimum. "So $40,000 up front, plus reimbursement for out of pockets."

The money didn't change his odds, but it was attractive. *What's the downside?* he thought. "What happens if you change your mind after two weeks?"

"Then you've got $40,000 to help you kick back for awhile," Jack responded.

"It'd have to be above board. No sneaking around, looking through somebody's files, pretending I'm on official business."

Jack nodded.

Ralph continued processing the offer. It would be a nice down payment for an extended leave. He doubted they would make any progress in that short a period, but Jack was calling the shots, and it was his money.

"Okay. I'll work with you, subject to some ground rules."

"Fire away," Jack said.

"First, I clear this with JAG, so I don't get myself or you caught in a wringer. I don't see a problem, but I've learned to ask."

"Agreed."

"Second, I won't engage in any attack on the Corps. No threats, no charges of a cover-up, nothing like that."

"Agreed. I'm not interested in the institution."

"The two may conflict," Ralph challenged. "I'm not optimistic, but we may discover a closer look should have been taken at your brother's death. Or that things were sloppy. There might not even be an investigative record. Regardless, I won't sign up for that as the basis for an attack, even if they screwed up."

"Okay," Keane agreed. "But say we turn up some evidence against one or two Marines? Does confronting them violate that condition?"

"Carving out a bad apple is fair game, if it comes to that. Third . . . ," Ralph began.

"Whoa," Jack interrupted. "How long is the list?"

"And final. At any point I think we're spinning wheels, I exit without hard feelings. Even if four weeks hasn't elapsed. And without a refund."

■   ■   ■   ■

The rest of the week flashed by as Jack worked on three fronts. By the weekend, he was stretched.

He summarized his initial Quantamica efforts for Roland Haskins and his partners. The quick read highlighted senior leadership too concerned about titles and entitlements and not focused enough on growing the business profitably, all in the wrapper of an immature organization and naïve CFO. His instincts signaled foolishness, not fraud, at the root, but he had lingering doubts. The quality of sales coming from their Asian affiliate was an open question. More legwork, including a trip to Hong Kong, face to face meetings with local leadership and some customers, was needed.

At the same time, Jack arranged bridging coverage for Impact Consulting. He wasn't sure how long he'd be out of pocket, and couldn't leave a client that needed quick assistance hanging. Any calls that required immediate triage he'd refer to a close associate.

Finally, he and Ralph invested two half-days developing their plan of attack. First, they'd exhaust all accessible information sources, including National Archives, U.S. Navy Records and any other repositories that made sense. From that initial search, they'd prioritize leads for further development. Third was field work—face to face visits. Their approach wasn't serial. Each leg would move forward as fast as they could manage.

In that first late afternoon meeting at Jack's condo, they stated three hypotheses. First was suicide, possibly drug induced, the official explanation.   Next, accidental death.

They couldn't define precisely what that meant, but they knew they needed to allow for it. Finally, homicide.

Both the accidental death and homicide scenarios had branches, including drug dealing and other criminal activities. The coloring might get clearer as they moved deeper into the investigation.

Each factoid they uncovered would go into inventory, hopefully giving credence to one of the three, channeling their efforts and moving them closer to the truth.

They needed a cover story for their interest in a thirty-five-year-old death. Instead of spotlighting any particular angle, they'd say the Keane family wanted to establish if there was any basis to appeal to the Marine Corps to add Daniel's name to the Vietnam Veteran's War Memorial in Washington, D.C.

CHAPTER TEN

Northwest Airways flight 627 touched down in St. Louis ahead of schedule. Ralph was pleasantly surprised, given the flight from Reagan National connected through Detroit, and he expected delays. Briefcase and overnighter in hand, he was at curbside in a cab in fifteen minutes.

"Naval Records Center, 9700 Page Avenue," he instructed the driver.

"You don't need a cab," the young man protested. "Catch the bus. It's a short run from the airport. You can practically walk there."

Ralph smiled. "I know. Six point seven miles. The sooner we get going, the quicker you're back for a better fare, right?"

The cabbie looked ready to respond with something rude, but after inspecting the tall man in the rear view mirror, he hit the meter and pulled into traffic.

Ralph was in civvies. His service uniform with gold oak leaves might make things easier at the Navy facility, but he was on leave.

■　　■　　■　　■

The night before, Ralph visited Ed Stanley at his JAG office. He told his friend he was accepting Keane's offer of a short-term assignment.

The lawyer was surprised. "Doing what?"

"Helping him look into the circumstances of Corporal Keane's death."

Stanley studied his friend, apparently about to say something, then instead rose from his chair, turning to face the window.

"What's the arrangement?"

"I agreed to consult. Weekly rate, four week minimum."

"See any conflict between consulting and remaining on the active list while you're on leave?"

"No. Anything I do is as an independent contractor, not a Marine officer."

Ed Stanley sat down at his desk, rotating to again face the window, and put his feet on the sill. He silently considered things in that oblique posture for a minute.

"That's a new one, but then again, it's not up to me. You aren't here for permission. You came here for . . .?" Ed left that floating in the air, somewhere directly above his head.

"Advice."

"You could ask permission formally through the chain of command. Got a problem with that?"

"I've developed a habit, counsel, of asking permission as a last resort. I'd rather not, unless it's absolutely necessary."

"Better to apologize ex post facto than be denied?" Ed returned to an upright position in his chair, swiveling to face his guest.

"Something like that. Anyway, any red flags?"

"Nothing obvious." He paused, pursing his lips. "It might get you in a sticky discussion about how you spent your summer vacation, but I don't see serious risk of collateral damage, like to your pension."

"Thank you, counsel, for that friendly advice."

"That is," Stanley continued as he took Ralph's extended hand in his own, "unless you end up really pissing someone off, Agent 007."

■   ■   ■   ■

After settling with the surly taxi driver, Gutierrez walked up the stairs of the Naval Personnel Records Center entrance. Signing in at the security desk, he presented military ID and asked the guard if he could check his overnighter.

"Absolutely, sir. I'll keep it here."

"Thanks. Can you buzz Ms. Whitaker, let her know I'm here for our eleven o'clock?"

The guard put through the call. Five minutes later, the access door in the right corner opened, and a brunette, five feet six, perhaps forty-five years old, entered the waiting area. Abby Whitaker extended her hand.

"Pleased to meet you, major. Follow me." They went through the same door, down a hallway, hard right, and entered a windowless office arranged simply—desk facing the wall, small round conference table, two chairs, potted plant, framed Ansel Adams photo, no other pictures. She motioned Ralph to a seat at the table.

"Coffee?"

"Please; black." She sent for the coffee and joined him at the conference table.

"Thank you for meeting with me, Ms. Whitaker."

"It's Abby," she interjected. "I appreciate the advance notice, and retrieved Corporal Keane's service file. We need to cover some housekeeping items, all right?"

Ralph nodded.

"The file's available to next of kin or their authorized representative. I got the faxed copy signed by David Keane," she said, referring to the file in front of her on the table, "father of the deceased. I need the original with the notary's seal."

Ralph took it from his briefcase and handed it over. Next he presented government ID in duplicate as the coffee arrived. Abby handed it all to the assistant, asking for copies. Returning to her guest, she referred again to the checklist atop the file.

"Is the family's request for access part of a formal document discovery action?"

Ralph looked perplexed.

"Your access to Corporal Keane's service file won't be affected by your answer. But if there's litigation involved, it affects the procedures we follow."

"It isn't a legal action. Corporal Keane's family wants to know the details surrounding his death. The information conveyed to the father in 1968 wasn't extensive. He may appeal for his son's name to be added to the Vietnam War Memorial, depending on what they find." He didn't feel disingenuous. For all he knew, they might end up making an appeal, though it was a long shot.

"Thanks for the clarification. Here's how our process works." After a two minute tutorial, he followed her down the hallway to the research room. Taking a seat at one of the four tables that covered most of the floor, he acknowledged receipt of the service record of Daniel Peter Keane, Corporal, USMC (Deceased). Abby then handed him the thick file, walked to the counter and had a short discussion with the duty clerk, nodding toward Ralph as she spoke.

Keane's file was fat for a single tour Marine. Opening it, he scanned the active duty summary: military occupational specialty (supply), training, assignments, awards, leave, disciplinary actions (none). Next came results from the battery of recruit aptitude tests, followed by pay history. Ralph noticing Keane banked most of his pay in Vietnam. *Either he was living cheap, or had another source of income,* he thought.

Perusing the rest of the thick file, Ralph internalized its organization and content. Proficiency tests—physical, marksmanship (expert with the M-14, M-16 and .45 caliber pistol)—came next, followed by promotion history. Paging forward, he hit an atypical section, one he'd seen twice before. Titled "Report of Investigative Inquiry," before him lay the official report of the corporal's death.

The standard *From, To,* and *Subject* headings were immediately followed by *Summary and Conclusions.* A list of supporting evidence, Exhibits 1-8, came next. The report was addressed to Colonel F. W. Martin, Commanding Officer, Headquarters Battalion, Force Logistics Command.

He read the two page summary. Keane's body was discovered by PFC Andrew Merrick, 8:05 A.M., 11 January 1968. In sterile prose, it reported the remains were partially recognizable, though the detonation of a fragmentation device at close range within the tight confines of a sand bagged bunker seriously mutilated the upper torso and head. On discovering the body, Merrick summoned appropriate authority, Gunnery Sergeant Eric Walters. He in turn requested medical and military police assistance. Attachments referenced statements from Merrick, Walters, a Navy corpsman and MP sergeant.

LAST EFFECTS

The corpsman estimated Keane was dead at least eight hours, based on blood loss and body temperature. Cause of death—wounds from detonation at close range of a fragmentation device, likely a hand grenade. The corpse was discovered in a bunker, one of many that dotted the camp, used to escape incoming fire. That specific bunker was close to but not part of the manned defense perimeter of Camp Books, Red Beach, Da Nang.

No hostile fire or VC/NVA incursion of Camp Books had occurred that night, and none of the perimeter posts in the bunker's vicinity reported suspicious or unexplained noise, e.g., a grenade explosion.

The investigating officer, Lieutenant Davis, discounted enemy action as cause of death, suggesting three alternatives: accidental detonation (unusual, but possible), suicide, or homicide. Ralph noted the investigator did not use the grunt vernacular, *fragging*, for the last alternative. After interviewing Walters and Merrick, however, the lieutenant concluded suicide was the cause of death. He referenced their statements regarding Keane's mental state since return from Okinawa. Also, substance abuse was cited as a probable contributor, supporting evidence of same discovered with the corporal's personal gear (one vial of pills, believed hallucinogenic). Signed and witnessed statements obtained from each of the personnel referenced in the summary followed.

The report was submitted to Colonel Martin on 17 January. Formal acceptance occurred 15 February, by Lieutenant Colonel Tighe, battalion executive officer, on behalf of the CO.

Before turning to the individual statements, Ralph jotted down top of mind questions. Why was Keane in that bunker? No one heard the grenade explosion? What changed after Okinawa—e.g., was his requested transfer to

CAP denied? Other evidence of drug abuse? Keane banked his pay, so how could he fund a drug habit? Was he dealing? Why the four week gap between investigative submission and acceptance?

The key investigative source was Sergeant Walters, who according to Keane's secret note was helping him get reassigned, smoothing things over with "the boys."

He decided to break for lunch. Returning the file to the clerk, he said he'd return in an hour.   There was a luncheonette midway down the block, opposite side of the street. Well past lunchtime, there was plenty of seating. He grabbed a remote booth and, after ordering, dialed Jack.

His update was delivered using their pre-agreed code for public communication.   Ralph initially resisted the suggestion as too cloak and dagger, but ultimately went along. "We don't know what we don't know," the consultant had argued. "Best to err on the side of caution."

"Completed a first pass on the client file. I'll take a second dip after lunch. There're questions I'll detail later. Still need to read the supporting statements and look closely at the timeline."

"Understood, Ralph.   On my end, I've hired additional talent, someone I've used before.   She'll start researching 'activities of interest' then in the host country, especially in the territory of our client."

Ralph finished his lunch, eyes watching traffic and the few pedestrians adjust to the sudden rain squall that moved in, mentally processing his first pass of the service file. Thirty minutes later, back in the research room, he signed the file out again.

"Signing it out is standard procedure when accessing a file?" he asked the duty clerk.

"When it's accessed by a third party—anyone not part of the records retention unit—either here or in the field."

"Can you tell me if Keane's file was pulled before?"

"Easy, starting in 1998." The clerk turned to a console, typed in some code, then shook his head. "No activity, major."

"What about before 1998?"

"That's challenging," came the reply. "Access records pre 1998 are paper, filed by year."

Ralph grimaced. Paging through record bins to see if the file was of interest before 1998 was a mind numbing prospect.

The clerk continued. "Miss Whitaker said you get the 'hot towel' treatment, major, seeing how you're family. I'll share a trade secret. When third parties request a file, the records team in the field or here typically notes the date, organization, and initials of the requestor on the inside rear flap of the jacket. Makes life a whole lot easier for everyone downstream if questions come up."

Thanking the clerk, Ralph settled in for round two. First up was the statement of Gunnery Sergeant Walters. The E-7, Keane's direct boss in Materials Company, signed his statement 13 January. He indicated Keane was a responsible lance corporal and logistics team member for the first half of his Da Nang tour. His dependability and mature judgment led Walters to recommend him for NCO school, a reward that positioned him for further advancement. Keane was promoted before departing for Okinawa in November 1967. But after he returned, the corporal went into a downward spiral—slovenly, surly (though not insubordinate), an attitude problem. Walters, per his statement, took Keane aside twice and gave him Dutch-uncle advice to get his act together. Instead, the situation regressed—late for duty, supply screw ups, slacking off. The E-7 suspected drug or alcohol abuse but never caught him with drugs or drunk on duty.

Parts of the statement replied to questions the investigating officer asked the sergeant. Yes, Walters considered an Article 15 for Keane for his shoddy performance, but he gave him a chance to square away. Keane was in that bunker because "It was familiar; it's right behind our main warehouse. And it's private—nobody's hanging out there, especially at night." Apparently prodded by his questioner, the sergeant then played the possible drug use card, though he admitted no direct proof.

PFC Merrick's statement was shorter, focused. He seconded Keane's withdrawal from the other men after returning in November. Also in response to investigator probes, Merrick stated he wasn't "certain" Keane did drugs. *Interesting word choice,* Ralph thought. The PFC had no idea what caused the withdrawal, wasn't aware of a girl problem, no "Dear John" he knew of. No particular confidants or enemies among the men.

Next up was the corpsman. Identification of the corpse was established via ID tags, one around neck, the other laced into the right boot. Body was transferred to the graves registration unit for processing and shipment home. One sentence was in response to a question—the corpsman had not taken blood samples from the bunker and matched them to Keane's.

Sergeant Mallory, MP detail at Camp Books, searched the corporal's personal area in the squad's hut on 12 January. Keane shared the space with nine other men, his rack area adjacent to the door. The MP discovered a vial of suspect pills in Keane's shaving kit, open on the shelf behind his rack. He queried two hut mates about the discovery. Both expressed surprise.

The rest of the file was typical detritus collected in an active tour of duty.

Ralph flipped to the back folder. Penciled in the inside flap, top left corner was "08JUN68; CIDFMFPAC; JL."

Why was Criminal Investigations Division, Fleet Marine Force, Pacific, interested in the death of Corporal Daniel Keane, six months after the fact, he wondered?

CHAPTER ELEVEN

Seated in Impact Consulting's conference room, Jack, Ralph, and Becky Wolfe were in a three way discussion. Becky, the researcher Jack brought on, was presenting her initial results developed in the last forty-eight hours.

"A lot was going on in Vietnam beside the war," Becky continued. "Number one on the hit parade was currency fraud, which Treasury estimated at $250 million— per year. That's more than half a billion in today's dollars, not chump change. It was equal opportunity fraud, everything from global networks to mom and pop operators. Most was illegal arbitrage, the big players converting Vietnamese piasters to U.S. dollars to gold for deposit in Dubai. Then there was your local PX cashier taking in local currency from the *mama-san* bordello operator, converting to dollars at the official exchange rate, pocketing a twenty-five per cent commission along the way."

Becky looked up from her notebook, providing space for questions. Hearing none, she continued. "In place position was drugs, also going gangbusters. Tough to establish direct connections to American military on the supply side. Our guys were a big factor in local demand, but I haven't turned up direct U.S. personnel involvement in the distribution network run out of South East Asia. That will require more work, if you choose to pursue it.

"Next comes procurement fraud. That's a broad category, with plenty of rackets within. One of the high octane scams was slot machine and juke box concessions, touching all the service clubs out there. Part of our export of free enterprise to the region, I suppose." Neither man smiled, and Becky got back on point.

"Turns out one company had an exclusive on that trade, including retaining fifty per cent of the profits. Their agent was buddies with some of the brass. That's *our* brass, not the local mahatmas. Congressional inquiries, some negative press, but it ran on until the war ran down." Jack and Ralph rolled their eyes but made no comment.

"A subplot in this category was the USO kickback scandal. Those responsible for booking acts were receiving cash kickbacks and other 'favors' (Becky used her fingers to put the quotes on that) from entertainers.

"Last but not least"—Becky signaled wrapping up—"there's what I brand supply redirection. Material goes missing between initial manufacturer shipment and final receipt, redirected for sale in the local market or exported to a third country. Covered everything from pallets of Coca Cola to night vision scopes for tanks. A cornucopia of marketable material, lax oversight and cash customers—all the makings of some old fashioned larceny."

Becky sipped her coffee. "My segmentation is a bit artificial. But I found it useful to organize the material."

"Artificial?" Jack queried.

Becky took a moment. "Investigative materials from that period—from Congress, the armed forces, Treasury Department—indicate criminal activity that involved U.S. personnel was often organized geographically. A ring of military, U.S. civilians, and like minded locals would organize in Saigon, get involved in black market currency trading, branch into procurement kickbacks and ultimately outright theft of supplies." Becky paused for another swig of coffee.

"There were synergies. Stolen supplies sold for piasters got parlayed into fatter profits by conversion to dollars at the official exchange rate, 118, instead of the black market rate of 200 per dollar. A double dip."

"Any typical configuration to these larceny rings?" Jack asked.

"Pretty much as you'd expect. Had to have some officer involvement for air cover, to keep out unwanted scrutiny. Well placed logistics talent—supply sergeant types that knew the ins and outs of the chain, what might trip an investigative wire, what would pass below the radar. Throw in a dash of lower level muscle, to do the grunt work—load the truck, drive the fork lift, that kind of thing."

"Where did Da Nang fit into the Marine's supply chain?" Jack directed this to Ralph.

"It was the hub. Our guys were in the bulls-eye, out there on Red Beach."

.   .   .   .

Ephraim joined Jack and Roland Haskins at Morton's Steak House in Vienna, a short run from Impact's office and on Roland's route from his D.C. office to Great Falls home.

Jack and Ephraim had talked earlier about their Quantamica assessment. The CPA ran twelve months of transactions through his forensic software. While nothing blatantly fraudulent popped out, the top executives were living well on the investor's nickel, including top-of-the-line leased cars, private club memberships and other executive welfare. It demonstrated less regard for investor cash than they accorded their own wallets. But these individual failures of frugality didn't explain the higher cash burn than expected.

The cash crisis had three roots. Two were quantitative, the last qualitative. Quantamica was pouring more cash into product development and support than budgeted. In parallel, receivables ballooned to five months of sales, two to three times the norm. While they were hitting on all cylinders in selling, they weren't collecting fast enough, especially in Asia. Those twin peaks of cash demand explained most of the cash drain. The qualitative root was focus. The CEO viewed the cash crunch as a financial sideshow, not the main event.

The company fell back on its cash reserves and bank credit, replacing the funds it was spending but not collecting from customers. That would carry them for a while, as they tapped their investors for new money. Their request had triggered Roland's earlier call.

Jack reserved a private dining room. Once settled, drinks served, dinners ordered, they turned to business.

"The place is run like a division of a big corporation," Jack kicked off. "The atmosphere still feels like Kimball—so long as they're profitable, everything is okay. They can call the parent company treasurer if they run out of cash. It hasn't registered that it's a stand-alone business." Jack cited support for the headline comment, including the CEO's lack of alarm, the CFO's inexperience in a separate company setting, unlike the womb of Kimball. "Both aren't comfortable engaging their peers on driving cash flow."

"Okay. What else?" Roland prodded. Jack knew his client had recruited the CEO, so it had to be going down hard.

"The chief technology gal is competent, but she'll bail out in the next sixty days if she doesn't get positive vibes. They're throwing more cash at the existing products than planned—client support, software patches and the like. We talked one on one, and she told me she's being set up, that it isn't the 'surprise' that the others are making it out to be. Also tells me that they've had problems stabilizing the software for the last six months. She sees where it's heading with no course correction. 'One hangs, the rest go free—only I'm not going to be the one who gets hung.'"

"She sounds like a keeper," the investment manager inserted.

"Operations and marketing are safe pairs of hands. Finally, the sales head. Either he's not exercising oversight or he's part of a bigger, non-kosher issue. I need more insight on that last point, and I'll come back to it in a moment."

Conversation ceased while salads and entrees were served. "Incentives are another issue, Roland," Jack resumed. "The top execs and sales team are motivated to grow the business, understandable given your objective to increase scale. But it's too weighted on sales and not enough on cash." Roland nodded.

"Back to development and support spending. The last product release was premature, and they're paying the price. Throwing bodies at product issues, holding customer's hands, redoing botched installations, and it's all costing cash that wasn't planned." Roland attacked his steak savagely.

"That brings us to receivables," Jack concluded. "Which explains half the additional cash they requested. Best case, you have a naïve incentive plan, lax oversight by the sales head and CFO. At worst, a subset of your senior sales folks, maybe some others, are goosing up sales to line their pockets."

"Channel stuffing?" Roland laid his fork down.

"Don't know. Needs more work."

"I may have funny business going on." Roland made it a statement, not a question, thinking about the implications.

Mouth set, he continued. "Okay, what do I do? Drop in a team and surround it, establish the facts, do damage control?"

"That's one way to go, Roland. We have an alternative. Instead of the surround strategy, insert your own person that you bolt onto the top team. Explain to your CEO that it's additional, unsolicited support from Rock Creek. Have the shadow work through these issues side-by-side with the current executives. That will help you sort through the keepers and who to jettison as the picture clarifies."

Jack paused. Reading Roland's silence as agreement, he continued. "In parallel, we need to kick the tires in Asia. A field visit to Alex Chung, your affiliate's head, coupled with some customer visits."

Roland considered quietly, tossing his napkin on the table. "Do you have people lined up to do both pieces?"

"Yes. The executive shadow can be on site Monday."

"What about the trip to Hong Kong?"

"That piece I'll address personally," Jack suggested. "I have work that'll take me to Asia, and I'll build in a stop in Hong Kong."

CHAPTER TWELVE

"We need a roster, the guys who served alongside Daniel in Materials Company. Until we have that, we're practically flying blind." Ralph stood in the living room while Jack went to the kitchen for refills. They started at 8:30 with a working breakfast. "And we need an ad in *Leatherneck*. Put out feelers for anybody who remembers him."

"*Leatherneck?*" Jack asked as he set the coffee mug on the end table.

"A Marine monthly. With an outreach column, *Mail Call*, to link people up. Anybody who served with Corporal Daniel Keane, Materials Company, Force Logistics Command, Da Nang between April 1967 and January, 1968, please contact Jack Keane, brother, at blah-blah-blah..."

"What about CID? How do we run down why they were interested in my brother?"

Ralph had thought about that since discovering the notation. "That's delicate, Jack. I need the old boy network on that front. I'm comfortable calling in some chips, but I need to confirm our agreement. No pulling the Corps through the mud, right?"

Jack grunted, Ralph accepting that as affirmative.

"I'll get that going. Becky will locate people, once we have names?"

"Right."

.　　.　　.　　.

Ralph hung up the phone. Ed Stanley had accepted his invitation to meet later for a drink, but he pressed for an agenda. "Social or business, amigo?"

He had to be straight, but wanted a face to face. "Yes. How about five-thirty?"

"Thanks for the bump and run, Ralph. See you later." But he wasn't chuckling.

Gutierrez carved out squatter's rights at the office, setting up in the room adjoining Jack's. Impact's layout was simple, functional, and economic, with two private offices, a conference room and a reception area.

Ralph's next call went to Abby Whitaker. He was put through, exchanged pleasantries, then asked, "Do you have a few minutes, Ms. Whitaker?"

"Sure. And it's Abby, major. What can I do for you?"

"Then it's Ralph, Abby. I appreciate the help last week. I need some more."

"What is it?" She sounded hesitant, but it was a start.

"I need a Materials Company personnel roster from sometime between mid-1967 through early 1968. How do I get that?"

"Initiating a search is easy. All rosters up to 1995 are stored here. That's the good news."

He bit. "And the bad news?"

"Comes in three parts, unfortunately. First, the records from then are paper, so it gets awkward, digging through storage boxes. Second, our records were never one hundred per cent. Some were lost, some never came to us, probably still sitting in a warehouse in California or Okinawa. Final, we had a fire in the early 1980's, and some were destroyed."

"Thanks, Abby. How do I initiate a search?"

"You already have. Let's talk turn-around time. The request goes into queue, and it could take a month. We work these FIFO, first-in, first-out. When it comes to the top, I assign a researcher. Search time varies. We could go through a lot of boxes, or hit pay dirt quick. Given the gaps I shared, we may open a lot of boxes before we're definitive."

Ralph was quiet for ten seconds.

"Those time frames are a problem?"

"Yes," he replied. They were both quiet, Ralph processing options to justify an expedited search.

"Ralph, is it an official request? If so, I'll move it to the front of the line."

He considered lying. "I wish, Abby. But it's for the family." He'd just have to accept the delay. The downstream impacts intruded on his thinking. The roster was the best chance to generate leads! Telling Jack of the delay would be a real treat. How about earning the $40,000 advance... what was he going to do for the next four weeks? Abby interrupted his musing, thankfully.

"You said the family may appeal to get their son listed on the Wall."

"Yeah. They question that it was suicide."

"What do you think?"

Another opportunity to lie. He was still skeptical, but he chose to spin it. "I have my doubts. I'm not sure why Keane died." Ralph congratulated himself on a masterfully ambiguous construction.

"I see you've mastered bureaucracy-speak, major. Try telling me what you really think."

Ouch, he smarted.

"Fair point, Abby. I'm conflicted. I'm skeptical that there's anything new we can learn about Keane's death. And I'm convinced there's more to the story—I just don't know what."

The records supervisor didn't respond immediately. Ralph's brain wanted to keep talking, but his gut ordered silence.

"I'm applying department head discretion and putting an expedite on your request."

Ralph didn't expect that and was surprised into silence. Finally recovering, he thanked her.

"Not sure why I'm doing it, major. Maybe because you didn't try pulling rank. Maybe I have a heart for the father. Either way, I'll be back to you once we have something."

▪   ▪   ▪   ▪

Ralph cranked out the *Leatherneck* posting before he left for the District. It would make the next edition, due for release shortly.

He pulled through the Navy Yard gate at 5:20 P.M., parking a block from the Officers' Club. He found Stanley settled into a booth on the club's outer perimeter, pre-positioning them for privacy.

"¿Qué pasa?" Ed greeted as Ralph slid into the booth. The JAG lawyer had almost finished his draft.

"Mucho," Ralph rejoined.

Stanley studied his friend, clad in civilian attire. "Enjoying your leave? Spending all your time on the case of the dead corporal?" Asked with a smile, Ralph detected an edge.

"Mostly on it." Ralph chose *it* purposely, instead of case, investigation or other formal descriptor, avoiding any legally laden term.

"Well, at least it's generating pocket money. Anything of interest, or are you in the same place as when we last talked?"

"It's progressed. Had a peek at the corporal's service file, including witness statements on the alleged suicide. Interesting. The key statement is from the non-com mentioned in Keane's note, Gunny Walters." Ralph paused, signaling to the waiter to bring two drafts.

He used the interval for a thumbnail sketch of his trip to St. Louis. When the beers arrived, he continued. "I need your help." He waited for a green light, not sure what he'd do if it came back red.

"Go on."

"CID pulled Keane's file. Not sure what to make of that. I thought you might get me some G-2 on why they took an interest. You know, apparent suicide, combat theater, no apparent conflict. From your experience, what's CID's typical operating mode in that situation?"

"I don't know that there is a typical M.O., but so what? It's logical they'd pull a file involving suicide. Seems like good investigative blocking and tackling, right?" Ed took another pull on his beer.

"Sure. But they didn't pull the file until six months later. At the height of the action in Vietnam? Why the sudden interest in a suicide, a cold case, a Marine dead and buried half a year earlier?"

Ed considered, first studying the mug, then finishing its contents in a series of swallows. "They weren't interested in any suicide. Talk about a cold case, it would have grown hair by then. And the interested parties would be long gone, rotated home. They pulled Keane's file because another investigation was running, and your man's name came into it."

■   ■   ■   ■

Abby was alone in Section C, Building Six of the center, the first time she'd been back there since her promotion five years ago. Others were normally about, but it was Saturday.

After her call with Gutierrez, she planned to assign a senior researcher the task. But she soon discovered her dilemma. Her top candidate was flat out supporting a legal case that would stretch through at least another week, and that took precedence. Abby's backup candidate reminded her that *her* two-week vacation commenced at week's end, with a full plate until exit. Abby committed before securing her staffing, she realized belatedly. Either she called the major back and reset expectations, or… .

She was in the 1966-72 warehouse area, three hours into the Fleet Marine Force-Pacific (FMFPAC) records. Containers were stacked five across by two high per shelf, five shelves separating floor and ceiling. All fifty records containers had a contents label, but Abby knew she couldn't trust their accuracy. Her first scan found no mention of Force Logistics Command, so she started to march through individual containers. Popping each lid, she searched for any hint of her three targets: FLC, Headquarters Battalion, Materials Company. Now perched on the fourth step of the wheeled staircase, she balanced between the stair step and the steel shelf frame.

She sensed closing in on her target half an hour back, locating two thick folders for Force Logistics Command. Flipping through, however, she found nothing for Materials

Company. Chagrined, she took a break, heading for the rest room and vending machines.

Abby considered how to proceed as she got a Diet Coke. She had been through twenty-two containers, not quite half the universe. Walking back, no "a ha" insight struck. She committed to invest up to two more hours.

Remounting the ladder, she opened the next FMF container, immediately striking oil. The exterior label promised contents for 1st Marine Division, Detached Units, Various, but the guts included a folder titled Headquarters Battalion, FLC. "Got you, you rascal," Abby exalted for her own benefit, descending the movable staircase.

Laying the coveted file on a work table, she grabbed a folding chair and, sipping a second Diet Coke, reviewed the contents page by page. Pages were in reverse chronological order, 1970 at the front. Not trusting the sequencing, she went through the first dozen pages, all after her timeframe. When she hit 1968, she slowed down, taking extra time scanning unit designations, dates and names. Headquarters Battalion had multiple and fluctuating appendages, Abby noted, as units detached and new ones were bolted on. Turning from the Battalion Staff roster, she walked through Logistics, Services, and Maintenance Companies. And then came Materials Company, 30 June 1967, the personnel roster split between officers and enlisted, alphabetically. Her finger moved down enlisted names to the middle of the alphabet, finding *Keane, Daniel P., Lance Corporal,* right where he was supposed to be.

CHAPTER THIRTEEN

"We'll organize around three overlapping buckets," Jack continued, drawing circles on the white board. The graphic reminded Ralph of the three-ringed Ballantine beer logo of his youth.

He labeled the first circle "lead generation." Armed with the Materials Company personnel roster, Becky would take the lead locating anyone who knew Keane. There were 213 names as of June, 1967, including a dozen officers. Two had priority: Eric Walters and Andrew Merrick. Walters was on the roster. Merrick wasn't, which meant he came on board after mid-year.

Two other priority targets were the penciled references in the photo album: Mouchie and Rick L., the pals forever. "Mouchie has to be a nickname. No parent would burden their kid with that moniker." Jack was emphatic, and Becky agreed. Ralph was less confident, encountering as creative names during his military tenure.

For Rick L., Becky had two possibles: Richard Love, Lance Corporal, Materials Company, or a second possibility from the Platoon 2037 boot camp graduation book. Acquiring a copy using her research savvy, it was now part of their archive. Richard Lapin was in Keane's recruit platoon. Either could be their man.

Bucket two Jack labeled "CID." Ralph was lead. After their officers' club drink, he asked Stanley for entrée to the criminal investigations arm. The JAG lawyer grudgingly agreed to provide unofficial liaison.

"Field work" was the final, bifurcated circle, subdivided between U.S. and Asia. The Asia piece formalized Jack's intent to go to Da Nang. Skeptical, Ralph had discussed it with Jack the night before, in private.

.   .   .   .

"What are you going to accomplish touring an abandoned military base, thirty years after the fact? Everyone we're interested in is American, as far as we know. Can you even locate where the camp was? It may be a Club Med, or whatever."

Jack listened politely. "We don't know what we don't know. It's low probability, but it needs to be done. I've got the album photos. It's a long shot, but I may get lucky."

They went back and forth until Ralph realized the real driver. Jack had to visit the place where his brother's life ended. He wasn't confident Jack was self aware of his need. Tugging on that thread a bit more, he recognized that Keane had to assign some logic, even if flawed, to his action. Instead of admitting—recognizing?—that his heart was driving, he clung to what he knew was a thin rationale. The Da Nang trip wouldn't help answer "why?" But Jack had to see it, take in the landscape, the horizon, the sounds and smells of Red Beach.

Jack moved the conversation forward. "I want you to go with me." Ralph suspected that coming since their sail on the Potomac, and he was ambivalent. He had toyed with a return visit to Vietnam but never put wheels on it. If he did, it would be solo, he told himself. Nothing against veterans groups, he just wasn't into a group grope down memory lane.

Now Jack proposed a duo, tag team visit. He'd hit Hong Kong on the outbound leg, complete the Quantamica field work, then fly to Da Nang. They'd connect there. Jack had made the request, now Ralph had the ball.

He told Jack he'd sleep on it, give him an answer the next day.

When they got together first thing in the office, before Becky joined them, Ralph agreed to go, with an addition. He'd precede Jack by three days, incorporating a trip north to the demilitarized zone. Since he was going the 8,500 miles to Da Nang, he'd invest in a trek north to some of his old haunts.

■　　■　　■　　■

"What else do we need to cover?" Jack probed the group, shaking Ralph out of his reflections.

"How do I handle Walters when I make contact?" Becky asked.

"Say more," Jack requested.

"I'm working the phones, tracking down an ex–Marine with a fairly common name, and I plan to connect with our man. How do I play that? 'Congratulations, Sergeant Walters, you just won a free ginzo knife set, just answer the following questions.'"

"Sorry to be obtuse." The trio kicked around exit strategies for Becky. Everything rang hollow, so they reverted to their standby: the Keanes needed more information about Daniel's death, given the war memorial appeal angle.

"That may spook him," Ralph said.

Jack nodded. "Once Becky finds him, we'll have to confront him. Let's keep it simple, stick to our story. For now."

Ralph walked back to his desk. The voice mail light was lit. He returned Stanley's call. After a quick hello, the attorney got right to the point.

"Remember Abscam?"

"The name, but not what it was. Remind me."

"Back in the late seventies, FBI sting operation, targeting politicos to go on the take of a fictitious Arab company."

"Vaguely," Ralph replied. "Why?"

"It happens our CID friends invented their own sting in the late sixties. Target wasn't politicos, of course. No biting the hand that feeds you, what? It was U.S. military and government renegades in Vietnam. They set up a fake shell company, Da Lat Trading. Then passed the word that Da Lat was a world class 'expediter,' moving goods, currency, supplies, what have you, on a preferred basis. No questions, no complicated customs forms, no currency controls. Just a well connected company with friends in high places, facilitating things into or out of Vietnam."

"I get the picture. What's that have to do with Keane?"

"On the surface, nada. But when I asked my friend Captain Jack Stein, formerly CID, to take a peak at the Da Lat file, he found a couple of interesting tidbits."

Ed was going to drag it out, so Ralph had to play his part. "Such as?"

"Expanding our knowledge about criminal cases CID was spending time on during the go-go years of 1967-68."

"And?"

"And," Stanley paused for drama, "He came across Operation Shade."

"Operation Shade?" Ralph parroted.

"Who knows who makes up those names, but my guess is whoever came up with it was a Greek mythology fan. You remember your Greek mythology, Ralph?"

"Only the guy who kept pushing the rock up a hill, which is starting to feel familiar. Enlighten me."

"Well, when I studied Greek mythology at the Delbarton School, I recall that a shade was a phantom, the insubstantial remains of the dead. Interesting name, don't you think?"

"Very."

"That's factoid one. Now for part two. Guess who pulled Keane's service file for a look-see in June, 1968?"

"A CID investigator working Operation Shade."

"Bingo! Give the man a Havana. For some reason, CID out in I Corps linked your man, deceased January, 1968 to their Shade operation."

"Why?"

"Don't know. Captain Jack will go the next step, and try to locate further material through his contacts. Unofficially."

"No, sir. The Eric Walters I'm searching for was definitely in the Marines. But I thank you for your time."

"Is that it?"

"Yes. Thanks for returning my call," she concluded, disconnecting.

It felt like break time. Looking at her watch, it was well past lunch. She walked to Ralph's office. Jack was with him, discussing their trip. "Are you guys eating lunch?"

The men looked at each other, then Jack responded. "Hadn't thought about it."

"I have, and I need fuel. Anybody interested in joining me, or can I bring something back?"

"Take out sounds good," Jack answered. They settled on a restaurant nearby, Becky noting their orders. "This is a working lunch, so it's on me," Jack added, handing Becky a fifty. Ralph noted that was after they chose their entrées. After lunch, she returned to her list, keying in prospect eighteen.

He was on the patio when he heard the phone. He forgot to carry a portable handset outside, again. "Damn it," he muttered, then was up from the lounge chair and into the living room through the sliders. The caller ID displayed 703, and he was momentarily torn about picking it up. *Probably a sales call*, he thought, but then picked it up on an impulse.

"Yeah?"

"Eric Walters?"

"Speaking. And if you're selling something, forget it. I'm not interested."

Becky paused. "No, it's not a sales call. I'm settling an estate, and trying to locate Eric Walters, formerly of the Marine Corps."

He processed silently, trying to frame a reply that got more information than he gave. His best was "Who wants to know?"

"My client, Mr. Walters. We need to be sure we're talking to the right person. Were you in the Marine Corps?"

"Who's the client? Gimme a name. I need to know who I'm talking with before I give out private information." *Bitch* was almost tacked on.

"As I said, my name is Rebecca Wolfe. *When* were you in the Marine Corps, Mr. Walters?"

"If this is legitimate, have your client send me a letter. Sounds like bullshit to me!" He slammed the receiver down.

"What the hell was that all about?" he asked the room. "And why did you pick up the phone, dumb ass?"

.   .   .   .

"I think we found our man!" Becky exulted as she entered Jack's office. Ralph was footsteps behind as she took a seat by the desk. "Eric Walters of Jacksonville Beach, Florida."

"He confirmed it?" Jack asked.

"No, it's that he wouldn't say. My call caught him off guard. The second I mentioned the Marines, he went sub-zero. He could have easily gotten rid of me, just by saying he wasn't an ex-Marine. When I popped the question, he froze— you could feel it through the wire! Not that he was Mr. Charm School at the front end, but that's probably his typical demeanor. I hit a nerve."

Jack asked for an instant replay. She walked them through the call, line by line.

"So he wants a letter, huh? What should I do? Call him up and introduce myself? Let him stew, see if he tries to contact us?"

"Call him up now," Ralph urged. "Once he settles down, he'll run that number through reverse look up, connect it with Impact Consulting, then you. And then he'll know whose estate we're calling about."

"Agreed," Becky nodded. "He may not pick the phone up, but put him on notice you're Daniel Keane's brother. That may rattle him."

Jack dialed. After four rings, the answering machine picked up. "Sergeant Walters, Jack Keane calling. Corporal Daniel Keane was my brother. I need to talk to you. I'm waiting for your call." He left the number.

Eric Walters listened. "So, it's about the Eagle Scout," he said to the room.

CHAPTER FIFTEEN

Jack strode briskly toward the airport rental lot. He landed in Pittsburgh at 3:10 P.M. and needed to get on the road to Emporium, Pennsylvania, to make his appointment. He bypassed the rental counter, grabbing a car from the preferred queue. The directions on the passenger seat, seat and mirrors adjusted to his 46R frame, he followed the signs to the airport exit.

Rick Lapin would meet him in the lobby of the Ramada, west of the town center. It was a three hour run— part state roads, part Interstate 80, with a final twenty mile straight run on PA 120 into town.

◾   ◾   ◾   ◾

Becky's data mining skills, honing in on Lapin as the *Rick L.* of Keane's album, trumped her employer's instincts. Jack (and Ralph too) was convinced the initials belonged to Richard Love of Materials Company, but Becky reserved judgment. Proceeding methodically, she cross referenced the photo of Lapin, recruit Platoon 2037, to the snapshots in Daniel's album. One, a beach scene, pictured a tanner, thinner version of the newly minted Marine private. She focused on locating that Rick L.

Her effort paid off with a call back to one of her many messages. After establishing the man on the line was the former Marine, she put him on hold, then passed the call to Jack after a quick update.

"Hello, Rick. I'm Jack Keane, Daniel's brother."

"Well, I'm pleased to speak with you. Daniel said he had a younger brother. I know it's been a long time, but I want to say I'm sorry."

"Thanks. It has been a long time." Jack explained his purpose, his need to understand more about Daniel's Vietnam tour. He paused, giving Lapin a chance to talk.

"I understand, Jack. It's weird. I've spent more time thinking about Vietnam in the past year than in the previous thirty. Don't know if it's because we're at war again, or if I'm just turning introspective, but anyway . . ." he trailed off. "How can I help?"

"My brother's personal effects just came back. That's what got me focused on his death again."

"Just came home? Talk about a FUBAR. Where were they?"

He told what he knew. "There's a photo in his album that looks like you. On a beach, in Vietnam?"

"That's me, all right," Lapin chuckled. "I remember that shot. Danny and me were at China Beach, a short in-country R&R, half a day."

That was a first for Jack. *Danny*. Another indicator of the separate identity Daniel developed after leaving home.

"When was that, Rick?"

"Well, the exact date's a challenge, but . . . let's see . . . " Lapin scrolled through his memory silently. "Sure. It was mid-October, 1967. Right around my birthday. Your brother got a cake. We washed it down with some real tiger piss," he laughed. "Er, that's the local brew."

Jack needed to progress the dialogue in person. Not sure why, he sensed he'd miss something critical on the phone.

"Rick, can we get together?"

Lapin took his time. "Not sure how I can help, Jack. I'm sorry about Danny's death. I never had a brother, so I can't say I know how you feel. I just don't see what I can add, beyond telling some sea stories from boot camp."

Jack pressed. "Rick, I'd like to buy you dinner. I know meeting you face to face for an hour will help me a lot."

The urgency took Rick Lapin aback, but he went along. They agreed on the Ramada.

■　　■　　■　　■

Jack pulled into the hotel parking lot five minutes after seven. Traffic on I-80 had backed up with construction delays, the compression to a single eastbound lane extending the drive time twenty minutes.

He spotted Lapin at the pay phone in the compact lobby. Making eye contact, Rick nodded, finishing his call. "Okay, darling, I should be home by nine."

They shook hands, Jack noting Rick's firm grip. Five–ten, trim figure, full head of wavy gray hair, trim beard, Lapin wore a blue short-sleeve and denim trousers. "That was my wife. Wasn't sure if I missed you, so I checked home to see if you called."

Jack apologized, explaining the delay. He asked Rick to pick where to have dinner.

"Here's okay, or down the road if you like Italian?"

Agreed on the latter, they went to the parking lot. Lapin drove. They passed the short distance in casual chatter—Jack's trip from D.C., how long Lapin was married, kids, and so on.

Seated at *La Cirenuse*, Jack ordered red wine, Rick a beer. Jack thanked him again for meeting.

"Your brother was top shelf. It's nice to finally connect him with family."

"You went through basic together," Jack started.

"Yeah. We met that first day. Parris Island. Must have been ninety-five, degrees and humidity. We knew we had really stepped in it, standing there on that parade deck, sweat pouring from us. Your brother and I had simpatico. You spend time close together, you get to really know someone. Were you in the military, Jack?"

"No."

"Then we went to Camp Lejeune, infantry training. Another four weeks. Yeah, we spent a lot of time together."

"Then to Vietnam?"

"No, not right away. I went to heavy equipment school in Virginia. Danny got orders to supply school. We were disappointed. Went into town and tied one on."

"Why disappointed?"

Lapin paused, locating the emotional memory. "We were naïve. Thought the only job in the Marines was infantry, grunts. Never thought there were other jobs—cooks, drivers, supply, whatever—that are part of the deal. So we were disappointed. Like we weren't good enough for a line assignment."

"What happened then?"

"We got over it," Rick smiled. "Danny went his way, I went to Virginia, then out to California. Six months later, we're both in Da Nang. So we got together for a half day of in-country R&R."

"Why so short?"

"Well, it wasn't really R&R. We managed to get away and meet at China Beach, hung out for an afternoon."

Jack leaned closer to the table. "How'd he seem, Rick?"

"We weren't in top form, as I recall. Strange time, strange place. There was a lot going on, but we were part of a sideshow, not the main event. Danny and me were both gung ho, and it didn't feel right to be on the sidelines."

Rick paused, finishing his beer. "Your brother, though, had a coping strategy. Said he was going to transfer to a grunt assignment for the second half of his tour."

"Did he tell you anything else?"

"Not that I remember. We had a few beers, don't forget, so I don't have perfect recall."

"Did he seem depressed?"

Rick was surprised. "Depressed? You must be kidding. He was always upbeat, an optimist."

"Did he mention drugs?"

Lapin's face hardened. "No way. There was stuff floating around, but neither of us was interested." He folded his napkin deliberately, laying it beside his plate. "Jack, where are you heading? Why these questions about depression? Drugs? What's up?"

"Do you know how he died?"

"No. I went through *Stars & Stripes,* looking for guys I knew in the casualty list. I saw Danny's name that January. Didn't list the cause."

"Supposedly, he took his own life. That's what we were told."

"Committed suicide?" Rick looked stunned. "I don't get it. That's not the guy I knew," he said, shaking his head.

Both men let that sink in. "Did Daniel talk about the guys he was with, Rick?"

"Like I said, he didn't like being rear guard, support staff. Finally, I told him somebody had to do it, just like somebody had to operate heavy equipment. He said supply was worse than I knew."

"Did he say why?"

Lapin shrugged. "It wasn't just being 'in the rear with the gear.'" He smiled, recalling the expression. Then quiet, thinking, the expression stimulating his recall. "He said he had fallen in with a pack of gonads, or something like that. Then we had another beer."

"Gonifs is what he said, Rick." Jack pulled Daniel's note from his pocket and handed it to Lapin. "My brother was among thieves."

■　　■　　■　　■

Top Walters pulled into the first available spot in the office building lot in Orlando. He'd have to hustle inside and up to the ninth floor in three minutes. The Colonel was a stickler on punctuality.

"The Colonel" was Larry Evans, United States Army, retired. Walters first met him in 1963 when Evans directed an inter-service task force, standardizing procurement of "special services" in the Western Pacific. Sergeant Walters, then Okinawa based, was assigned to the joint team as a supply expert seconded by the Corps. He and Evans developed a tight relationship early. A street savvy non-com, Walters quickly demonstrated an ability to get things done without regard to rules, regulations, or scruples. He had a special talent for sniffing out Evan's desired outcome, then making sure it happened.

One challenge the task force confronted was to standardize gambling and entertainment concessions across military clubs in the region. That was a contracting potpourri, an eclectic mix of vendors, handshake agreements, and local incentive deals cut by club managers with suppliers.

Chaos spelled opportunity, and Evans hit hard, making it the poster child of Task Force Tiger, his name for the inter-service team. It was easy pickings, once Evans applied "institutional jujitsu" on local managers and base commanders. Their first instinct was to circle the wagons and maintain control, but the Colonel was masterful at focusing top down pressure—senior officers intent on the next star, inspectors general looking for new heads to mount on the wall—salted with well-planted rumors of looming congressional inquiry. He brought it all to bear in a barrage of harassing fire on local base commanders. That was the stick, applied without quarter, but he also gave them a whiff of the carrot, a cash stream to support construction and enhancement of clubs across the Pacific, as long as things got done his way. His stump speech to the top brass was masterful, ending with the promise of preferred suppliers, standard contracts and scale economies. "And," he'd close, "it provides you an ongoing source of funds to reinvest in *your* priorities."

He rolled up the Army, Navy, and Marine Corps clubs in short order. The Air Force alone held out. Despite Evans' political skills and concentrated fire, the men in blue fought a successful delaying action. "Those guys never play ball," he confided to Walters, "and they've got the nukes."

Midway through his Tiger assignment Walters tumbled to Evans' real objective. Procurement efficiency was the banner, the spin to deliver the stealth prize, which became clear as the sergeant ran the bid process for the club's gaming contract. He was to orchestrate an "arm's length" selection process, and presented it to Evans. The Colonel complimented him on the rigorous design, then told him which vendor had to win the franchise: Hong Kong based Far East Gaming.

Evans' buddy, a former Army officer who served with him in Korea, was the front for Far East. Well-dressed, well-connected Bobby Blankenship—"BB" to his friends—knew how to rig decisions. For Walters, it opened the door to a new dimension of supply management. Far East Gaming's exclusive contract consolidated a series of cash tributaries—proceeds from service club slot machines and juke boxes—into a massive cash river. Far East retained fifty per cent of the highly profitable deluge (after deducting expenses) as compensation for its equipment and services.

Everybody who counted gained. Local clubs got gaming equipment fast and hassle free; clubs got expansion capital, a critical assist as the military footprint in Asia expanded; top brass pointed to the standard procedures for managing sin products, placating Congress. Far East Gaming was especially happy, as they demonstrated lavishly and routinely to their key constituents.

Walters discovered a collateral benefit of centralized procurement: offshore banking. His boss suggested to BB that a "thank you" investment account be established for the sergeant. "Call it your retirement enhancement account, Eric," The Colonel opined. At the time, the $25,000 Far East deposited in his account felt like a lot of money, a major multiple of his military pay.

▪   ▪   ▪   ▪

That was more than forty years ago, Eric thought, as the elevator stopped at the ninth floor. That was the first of a number of special deposits to his supplemental retirement fund, as he and Larry Evans maintained their relationship throughout the build-up in Asia. The Colonel retired in 1970, but that didn't end their dealings. "Just changing uniforms, Eric. It'll be a sports jacket and tie now, a different title, but there's gold in them hills and no reason we can't be part of the action." And they were.

He pushed the button at Suite 907, heard the buzzer and entered. The Colonel sat at the inner office desk. Walters walked forward and shook his comrade's hand.

Sitting in a facing chair, the retired Marine noted another decade's wear on his mentor's face. He had seen him last in Tampa, was it 1994? The last years had not been kind to the old man. He crossed into that cohort of the elderly that radiated "fragile," as if too strong a handshake would shatter the bones of their fingers.

"You're looking good, Colonel."

"Better than some stiffs you've seen, I bet," Evans snorted. "But thanks for lying. Now you're looking well, Eric. The beach agrees with you."

"It does, Colonel. I like the salt air. It has medicinal properties, according to my mother."

"And you're drinking a better Bourbon than when we first met, sergeant. That's added years to your life."

He fixed Eric with that same piercing look. *So much for the pleasantries,* thought Walters. "So what's this about needing to see me on old business? Your call wasn't clear."

"I didn't want to get into specifics on the phone. You never know who's listening nowadays. It's about a call I got. Guy looking into his brother's death back in Da Nang. In my unit. You might remember, we called him the 'Eagle Scout.'"

"Vaguely. But so what? What's the big deal about him calling about the brother?"

"Well, Keane—that's the Eagle Scout—was a straight arrow, wouldn't leave things alone. I tried different ways to keep him in his box and out of ours, but he kept poking around, everything by the book, every pallet of beer accounted for... you know the type."

"Now I recall. Hence the nickname. Go on," Evans prodded.

"Well, I tried to nail it down when I sent him to Okinawa with a special delivery. Made sure some MP friends knew he was coming, and what he was carrying. But they missed him at Kadena when he got off the plane."

"Not one of your better operations."

"No, so I had to come up with another approach. And I did."

"As I recall, the kid ended up taking himself out, didn't he?"

Eric looked at Larry Evans, but detected no humor, no sarcasm, just a deadpan. "That's right, Colonel."

"So I ask again, what's the problem? You have a guy who wants to understand his brother's death. Just call him back, tell him what you know, and be done with it."

"It's more complicated than that. If the brother is like the Scout, he's calling for a reason. Something's developed that has him suddenly investing a lot of time. Just finding me had to take effort. It's more than wanting some words about his brother's death. He's on a mission."

Evans listened intently. "If you don't call him, he'll put his own meaning on that. What Marine wouldn't return a call to next of kin?" Evans paused for emphasis. "Don't give him a blank to fill in, Eric. Suck up your concerns, call him back. Stick to your story. If he wants to take it somewhere else, just close him out, politely. And don't give him ammo by losing that temper. No mistakes, okay?"

He didn't wait for an answer, rising from his chair. "Drop me a note after you connect with the brother. That it's done, case closed. And take care of yourself, Eric. We seniors need to watch our health."

CHAPTER SIXTEEN

Ralph ordered a glass of white wine to accompany his meal. He returned his seat to an upright position and raised the meal tray from the armrest. Seated at the window, the seat to his right was vacant.

After the steward removed the dinner tray, he relaxed with a coffee and chocolate, mentally reviewing his itinerary. United 951, Dulles to San Francisco; then Far Eastern Air 717 to Taipei; four hour layover, then Far Eastern 391 to Ho Chi Minh City; finally, Vietnam Air north to Da Nang.

He'd precede Jack by three days. A tourism visa was stapled in his passport. One question gave him pause when completing the visa application, "The purpose of his visit to Vietnam?" He settled on "sightseeing and relaxation," forgoing any mention of his prior visit.

Three books kept him company during the flights west. Ralph had weaned himself from fiction years before, realizing history, biography and other non-fiction served his desire for escape better than novels. First up was a book on the Middle East. Reclining, he switched on the overhead lamp and began reading. Within twenty minutes, he was asleep.

LAST EFFECTS

•   •   •   •

Jack left Hong Kong International Airport via the express subway, heading to the Kowloon Hotel, a twenty-five minute trip. He had been to Hong Kong before, but it was his first time through the new airport.

He'd meet Alex Chung for breakfast the next day, using the evening to acclimate to the twelve hour time change.

The flight out was productive. Connecting through Chicago, he used the time to prepare for his meeting with Chung, catch up on reading, and review the CID file.

They received that file the day after Ralph departed. Ed Stanley tried to reach Ralph on his cell phone, leaving a message that Captain Stein had the file, including materials on Operation Shade. The message ended with a question— would Ralph pick it up, or should they courier it to the office?

Gutierrez retrieved the message during his San Francisco layover, replying on Stanley's JAG extension. Keeping it brief, he asked that it be delivered to Impact's office. Then he called Jack. They considered faxing a copy to his Da Nang hotel for delivery on check-in, then rejected that as too public. Instead, Ralph would get a personal look three days thence. As a precaution against curious inspectors, Jack bound his copy in an Impact Consulting wrapper.

Opening the file, he perused the contents. The first page was a routing slip transferring the file from Fleet Marine Force, Pacific, to Headquarters, Marine Corps, in October 1973. Next came a single page, prepared by Captain Edward Kowalski, CID, FMFPAC, dated September 1969, summarizing the materials. Jack started there:

> Eleven criminal investigations were
> conducted by CID, FMFPAC over the period

commencing 1 July 1967 through 30 June 1969 centered on procurement and currency fraud. Each targeted United States military and civilian personnel engaged in criminal activity in I Corps, Republic of Vietnam (RVN). Multiple military and civilian sources, supplemented by intelligence received from United States government agencies (i.e., CIA, Treasury) identified suspect activities, procurement violations, misappropriation of government property and illegal currency trading and movement. Individual investigations centered on major U.S. military installations and civilian population centers in I Corps, especially Da Nang city, port and logistics support facilities and related operational bases/ staging areas. Of eleven (11) investigations initiated during this period, nine (9) successfully terminated with the arrest, trial and conviction of involved military and United States civilian personnel and/or host country co-conspirators. Five (5) active duty military personnel were tried, convicted and sentenced through military courts martial; two (2) United States civilians in support operations in RVN were tried, convicted and sentenced in U. S. criminal court actions; twelve (12) citizens of RVN were arrested and dealt with via local criminal procedures.

As he completed the single page summary, Jack confirmed that Da Nang was a hub of illegal commerce.

LAST EFFECTS

The rest of the thick file was a condensation of the eleven investigations—investigative targets, actions taken, status updates, and ultimate results during the two year period. He read through page by page, searching for references to Operation Shade, individual names, places, and the Marine units the investigations focused on.

The first half of the compendium dealt with currency fraud, including illegal arbitrage between the piaster and U.S. dollar. Jack discovered the first reference to the Marine base at Red Beach two-thirds through the file. Repeated instances of supply shipments gone missing from the depot—everything from pallets of C-rations, uniforms, beer and soft drinks up through fuel and individual pieces of heavy equipment—sparked a CID inquiry. They created their shell, Da Lat Trading, to penetrate the siphoning operation. In November, 1967, they advertised that Da Lat was seeking military hardware and supplies for re-export to third world clients. In December, they procured $35,000 worth of material, including fatigues, packaged rations, tobacco and alcohol. Working through one Tran Tong Ba, a Vietnamese with "special access" to military stockpiles, they consummated the first test transaction. Smelling an opportunity to roll up a major network, CID gave Ba their wish list for a second transaction, including foodstuffs, clothing, and specific equipment items—like Starlight night scopes.

Ba agreed to broker the deal on his standard terms (twenty-five per cent down, balance COD, settlement in U.S. dollars), with the proviso to exclude all combat supplies—such as the night scopes. His contacts would not deliver obvious war material which could benefit the Viet Cong or NVA. Despite Da Lat's repeated assurances that the supplies were for export, the list was scrubbed. Da Lat advanced Ba

$25,000 as down payment, envisioning a major sting that would roll up the network. Delivery was promised by 1 May.

The carefully structured operation then went wobbly. Deliveries were expected at Da Lat's warehouse in Da Nang city, but nothing came. May Day passed with no fatigues, no MREs, no Scotch, no Ba.

The report identified the sting operation, code named Shade, as one of two investigations that did not result in the arrest or conviction of either U.S. personnel or local citizens. The CID lead, Lieutenant John Lettman, was reprimanded for the $25,000 loss of government funds.

■　　　■　　　■　　　■

Before returning the bound file to his briefcase, Jack used the air phone to leave a message for Becky Wolfe, instructing her to add John Lettman to her priority search targets.

CHAPTER SEVENTEEN

Andrew Merrick requested that the library stock *Leatherneck* when he was relocated there in 1987. The acquisitions committee approved. California State Prison, Sacramento, houses maximum security inmates serving long sentences or those who are problems at other institutions. Andrew Merrick was both.

Incongruously, Merrick was proud of his military service, evidenced by his positive though sparse comments on the topic and the bulldog tattoo sported on his left forearm. He acquired "devil dog" in Oceanside, California one weekend liberty. The bad conduct discharge, which Merrick omitted from his oral history, was a second lasting manifestation of his service.

In the past, Andy embellished his exploits with an imagined Purple Heart, ignoring that blood shed in a combat zone is necessary but not sufficient for that award. The blood has to result from enemy action. Blood shed by PFC Merrick resulted from action with other Marines.

The private never made lance corporal, even with a year of Vietnam service in the Force Logistics Command. He had a knack for screwing up and getting caught, and the petty skirmishes, drinking, and quickie AWOLs gradually escalated

111

to longer periods of absence without leave. His litany of Article 15s graduated to Captains Masts, and finally, after rotating stateside, a court martial. The skirmishes with authority culminated in a bad conduct discharge, also known as "six, six, and a kick"—six months forfeiture of pay, six months in the brig, and a boot out of the service.

The return to civilian life was eventful. Released from the brig at Camp Lejeune, North Carolina, he headed west, doing menial jobs of two to three week duration until he was fired or moved on.

He tumbled to what looked like a viable breakout strategy during a two day lockup in Albuquerque. In for assault on a vending machine at an all night truck stop, his cellmate was a serious crime veteran. "Take it from me, Devil Dog, if you're going to steal, at least make it worth your while. Remember what Willy Sutton said when they asked him why he kept robbing banks? 'Cause that's where the money is, Nimrod.' Not in vending machines." That jailhouse counsel struck a chord with Andy, resolving to apply it soon.

Crossing into California after his release, he searched for a suitable opportunity, armed with a .45 caliber pistol purchased in Flagstaff.

The target selected was a mid-point between vending machine and bank, at least in Andy's convoluted reasoning. It looked low risk and promised ease of execution. Instead of the typical late night liquor store heist, Merrick picked a combination gas station and convenience store west of Barstow at three-fifteen in the afternoon. After filling up, he went in as if to settle up for the gas. He asked for a pack of Kools, doing a quick 360 degree sweep of the store. Seeing no one except the middle-aged counter clerk, he put a ten dollar bill down, grabbed his cigarettes, and pushed back through the screen door.

"Wait a minute, son. You still got change coming," the clerk called after him. Andy looked up and down the highway, seeing no traffic. He went back in, pulling the .45 from under his shirt flap and faced the man, the pistol pointed at his chest.

"Open the cash drawer and put the money on the counter!" he screamed. The clerk started moving and talking at the same time.

"Okay, young fella, I don't want any trouble, you take it all, ain't my store anyway, just take it easy." The words poured from his mouth as he fumbled with the cash drawer, got it open and started clawing bills from the trays and throwing them on the counter. First the twenties, then tens. He attacked each bill pocket serially, maintaining a jabbering backdrop throughout. "No trouble, there's the twenties, moving as fast as I can, don't shoot me, please."

"I will shoot if you don't move faster!" Andy yelled. The clerk's hands moved back toward the cash drawer, but the shaking became spasms. The terrified hands flapped around the five dollar sleeve but couldn't grasp the bills, beating the air over the drawer as if jolted by electric shocks.

"Move it, damn you!" Andy screamed again, stuffing bills into his pocket with his left hand.

That's when the 1968 Chevelle pulled up to the pump nearest the store, the front tires hitting the ground cord and hanging a distinctive *Bingbing!* in the station air. The situation deteriorated quickly. Andy turned toward the sound as the clerk sank deeper into his rambling monologue. The Chevelle faced west. The driver got out on the far side, away from the store. Merrick, his eyes darting back and forth between the blubbering clerk and the gas pumps, saw a uniform hat. He panicked.

He turned back to the clerk, hand motioning the spastic to back away from the counter. The scarecrow, arms and hands flapping like straw in a light breeze, kept babbling while emptying the change drawers, slamming handfuls of coins onto the counter, oblivious to Andy's signal, aware only of his task.

The driver finished fueling and replaced the pump handle. Andy heard steps rounding the car and approaching the screen door. Taking a step farther back into the shadow, the ex-Marine pivoted to his left and, as a uniformed arm pulled the screen door open, fired. The bullet smashed into the surprised young man's face. His police cap flew upward as his body, struck by the large, slow velocity bullet, reversed from the doorway. He was large, over two hundred pounds, and his right hand retained its grip on the screen door as he fell backwards, pulling it from its hinges.

Turning back to the counter, Andy stared at the scarecrow clerk. He sighted on the chest of the paralyzed man before him. The hands ceased their wind milling, the clerk now calm. The instinct to continue the action, to squeeze off another round, was powerful, almost reflex. Yet something stopped Merrick's index finger from putting that final pressure on the trigger, instead lowering the pistol. Snatching the remaining bills, he ran through the now screen-less entrance and climbed back into his car, still parked at the pump.

He made it thirty miles west on Route 66 before being caught. Had witnesses not been present as he was cuffed and slammed into the back seat of the police cruiser, he would have been killed while resisting arrest, though he offered no resistance.

The homicide led to a life without parole sentence. Andy spent the next thirty-three years in three different California prisons. The first twenty-three were hard, as he continued to show *attitude*, although that dissipated with time. He learned how the system, both those in charge and the peer group, confronts and tempers attitude.

The last ten years were easier sailing, as he accommodated to institutional routine. Five years ago, Andy found Jesus, and though society hadn't forgiven him, Jesus had. From that belief came an armistice, then a reconciliation with his surroundings. He learned to accept, if not enjoy, life inside.

The latest issue of *Leatherneck* was in its familiar cradle in the prison magazine rack. After reading an article about the Corps' experiences in the Persian Gulf, he scanned Mail Call, part of his normal routine. Halfway down the column, his eyes riveted on the bold typeset word string—Keane, Force Logistics Command, Red Beach. Looking up, he thought about painful memory fourteen, so labeled in his meditations. Then he said a prayer for guidance.

CHAPTER EIGHTEEN

"Eric Walters, returning Keane's call," he announced to the female voice.

"I'm sorry, sir, but Mr. Keane isn't available. Can I take a message?"

"When will he be available?" He felt his pressure rising. He had rehearsed the call fifteen times, and he wanted it done.

"Are you a client, Mr. Walters? Or is it a personal call?"

"Personal."

"I don't expect Mr. Keane in the office for the rest of the week. I can have him call you when he returns. Can I take your number?"

His blood pressure rose further. "So he's unreachable? You can't get a message to him? Is there a place on the planet that doesn't have phones?" His words ended on a high pitch.

Yvonne of ProStaff Answering Service belatedly realized she was dealing with a Type A, cubed. "I apologize for any inconvenience, Mr. Walters. I can try to get a message to him. Since he's traveling internationally, I'm not certain when he'll return your call."

LAST EFFECTS

Once he heard "traveling internationally," he calmed down. That sounded important. "I see," he stalled, lowering his voice. "Then ask him to call me as soon as possible. Do you know the time difference between him and me?"

"I don't know, sir. He's in Hong Kong."

"Is he there for the week? Maybe I should try calling his hotel?"

She hadn't been instructed to share any contact numbers, so she took a message.

Why is Keane traveling in the Far East, he wondered? *Is it just that consulting crap he sells, or is he up to something?*

■   ■   ■   ■

The Vietnam Air flight into Da Nang had a surreal quality for Ralph. His memory retained the mental snapshot registered at the top of the boarding staircase to his flight out in 1969. F-4 Phantom jet fighters on the flight line, loaded with ordnance, ready to head out on missions. C-130 transports along the runway aprons, being serviced by ground crews. A military charter flight awash with replacements, their state-side fatigues still fresh. Deep half moons of perspiration soiled the armpits of Ralph's khaki blouse then as he entered the cabin of the outbound transport.

That was the case again, he noticed, feeling the moisture beneath his armpits. Thank God, he wasn't wearing khaki, so the perspiration rings weren't obvious. The jet cabin was comfortably cool as they taxied to the terminal. He couldn't fault the temperature.

Disembarking, he moved with the other passengers toward the security point. He cleared customs and passport examination in Ho Chi Minh City and didn't realize he'd run another official gauntlet in Da Nang. He was surprised when

117

the uniformed official signaled him to step out of line for an impromptu inspection.

He had a carry-on in his left hand, his briefcase in his right, and put both on the counter. "Passport," a second inspector requested. Handing it to number two, he turned back to the baggage inspector. The search was thorough, including flipping through the books and papers in his briefcase.

"Do you declare anything?"

"No."

"How long do you stay in Vietnam?" The question came from number two, holding the passport open.

"Six days."

"Where do you stay?"

"Da Nang Hotel." Ralph picked it for sentimental reasons, a significance he hoped was lost on these two. They looked too young. The Da Nang Hotel was a U.S. military haunt during the war, and he had been there before. It wasn't top tier, but that was okay. He wasn't there on holiday.

"Purpose in Vietnam?"

"Tourism, sightseeing."

"You come here before as GI?" The question was delivered with a smile, but Ralph was unconvinced.

"Yes, many years ago."

"Welcome again. Enjoy visiting our country. Much nicer than last time, you see." He collected his bags and headed for the street exit. A throng of taxi drivers and others hawked guide services and transport. Singling out an older driver, he handed the Vietnamese his overnight bag. "Speak English?"

"Yes, yes," he nodded, taking the bag with his right hand. He stepped in front of Ralph and opened the taxi's rear door. Ralph had to catch himself. He half expected to see an old French Citroën. "Please, please," the taxi man indicated, sweeping Ralph into the rear seat with the waving motion. His overnighter occupied the jump seat next to the driver.

"You go hotel?" the driver asked, looking at his American passenger.

"Yes. Da Nang Hotel. Dong Da Street." The choice surprised the Vietnamese, but he started the taxi and pulled out from the curb.

"You call me Minh, okay?" the man asked, smiling at Ralph in the rear view mirror.

"Okay." He was reminded how eyes can smile. "Call me Ralph."

"Mr. Ralph, very good," Minh repeated. "You like my taxi, yes?"

"Yes, it's nice. How far to hotel, Minh?"

"Not far. Maybe half hour. Da Nang Hotel old, not number one, Mr. Ralph," Minh offered, making eye contact in the mirror again, searching for any sign he offended. "Why not number one hotel, like Fujami Resort?"

The use of "one" and "ten" to define quality was familiar. "I was there before, years ago."

"You were soldier then?"

"Many years ago."

"Minh too. Captain Minh, Vietnamese Army."

"Which army?" Ralph asked.

"Ha, ha, very funny. South Vietnam Army."

The driver took his right hand off the steering wheel and fished in his pants pocket. Pulling his wallet out, he extracted a beaten black and white photo with one hand and passed it back. A younger Minh stared up, uniformed in tiger striped fatigues as a South Vietnamese captain. The man's propensity to turn and look at his passenger instead of the road ahead was a bit nerve wracking. "Nice picture, Minh." He handed it back.

They traveled a mile in silence, then Minh asked

Ralph's plans. Was he with a tour group? Did he have a guide already arranged? How long was he in Da Nang?

"Maybe Minh be tour guide? Inexpensive. Take you everywhere: Cham Museum, Marble Mountains, China Beach. Yes?" Minh's eyes focused through the rear view mirror, hoping.

Ralph considered. He was a good driver, despite the tendency to focus on passenger *and* highway. And he preferred throwing business to a former ally rather than a NVA or Popular Front type. The taxi, a Toyota Race, was roomy and looked rugged enough for some excursions outside the city. "How much?"

"Very reasonable. Forty dollar and Minh show all special places in Da Nang, yes?"

"No, not okay. But forty dollars for all day, including trip to Hue, Cua Viet okay," he countered.

Minh looked in the mirror. "Not possible see Hue, Cua Viet in day. Take two days, Mr. Ralph. Forty dollar no good." Minh's voice was firm, not whiney or pleading.

"Okay, forty dollars each day. We see Hue, Quang Tri, Cua Viet, then back to Da Nang."

They agreed to start at eight the next morning. Taking his overnighter, he walked into the hotel.

■   ■   ■   ■

Jack expected a call from Alex Chung at 8:30 A.M. from the lobby. He showered, had two cups of coffee, watched CNN Headline News, and read through the *Financial Times* by nine, with no sign of his host. Finally, he called Chung's office. The secretary asked to take a message.

"My name is Jack Keane. I was to meet Mr. Chung for breakfast. We confirmed last week, yet I haven't heard from him."

"I apologize, Mr. Keane. I was about to call you. Mr. Chung just called. Unfortunately he has an emergency and is unable to meet today. He apologizes for the inconvenience."

Brilliant, Jack thought. *Now my lead contact is missing in action.*

"I'm sorry, Miss . . . ?" Jack hesitated.

"Miss Ng, Mr. Keane."

"Thank you, Miss Ng. Did Mr. Chung say what kind of emergency? Is he okay?"

"He said it was personal. I do not know more. May I make any arrangements for you today, Mr. Keane? Would you like a tour, or dining reservations?"

"Do you have a number for him? Maybe we can talk by phone today?"

"Of course. I will give you his private number. But he told me he is not available, Mr. Keane, so you may not have success. Here is the number."

"Thank you," Jack replied, writing on the room service menu. "Assuming we don't speak today, is his plan to meet me for breakfast tomorrow?"

"Yes, I believe so. If Mr. Chung calls again today, I will confirm that. Goodbye, Mr. Keane."

Talk about the inscrutable East, Jack wondered. *What is this?* What personal emergency trumped their meeting, a meeting he came eight thousand miles for? Was it a stall? What difference could twenty-four hours make, if that was Chung's game? It made no sense.

He thought about a call to Quantamica USA's headquarters in San Francisco, but given the time difference, those guys were long gone from the office.

"Okay," he resolved out loud. "Let's take it one step at a time. First, breakfast."

▪   ▪   ▪   ▪

LAST EFFECTS

Becky Wolfe covered the home front, Impact's Tysons office. In addition to generating leads, she screened messages forwarded from ProStaff, relaying to Jack any that merited attention. She also checked for important mail.

They had agreed to use the office voice mail system, allowing both men access whenever opportunity presented. Her heads-up to Jack about Walters' return call sat in his voice mail queue.

She had no success putting a name to Mouchie. Richard Lapin didn't recall it from their boot camp platoon. Her single success with the Materials Company roster to date was Walters, and her call with him hadn't allowed for follow-up questions about Mouchie or anyone else. The search for Andrew Merrick was a dry hole also—too many Merricks, too little time. John Lettman, Jack's new addition to her priority list, hadn't received her attention yet.

Rifling through the office mail, Becky did her daily triage, much of the material immediately reaching escape velocity via the trash container. Authentic mail was opened and, if routine, went into the dated file for Jack's return. Time sensitive went into the red file, discussed when they made contact.

A letter sized envelope—hand addressed in block lettering, California postmark, stamped versus metered, no return address—got her attention. Carefully slitting it open, she found a single page, written in the same hand:

Mr. Keane,

I read your Mail Call. I knew Daniel. We were in Vietnam together. He was a decent guy, even though I didn't know him well. I'm sorry he died that way. It must

have been hard on your family. I pray for
God's peace on you the way it's on me.

Sincerely,

Andy Merrick

p.s. I have not led a very good life, and I've
been punished. I take peace in God's
forgiveness. I don't know if your brother was
a believer, but I hope so.

Andy Merrick, formerly PFC Andrew Merrick,
USMC. California postmark. The tone plus no return address
spelled prison, maybe not now, but at some point.

She left Jack a second message, copying Ralph. "Boss,
we have a reply to our *Leatherneck* troll. From Andrew
Merrick. Reads like he's done time. No return address, no
contact details. Says he's sorry about Daniel and the way he
died. Also sounds like a born again Christian. I'll work it.
Call when you can."

"Okay, let's get the heat seeking missiles going," she
said out loud, breaking the silence. "Andy Merrick. Let's look
for a violent crime, California, say 1968 to 1990." She started
cranking the search engine, narrowing, filtering, sifting.
Within thirty minutes she was reading the April 12, 1970
account of the robbery/homicide outside Barstow in the *Desert
Dispatch*. A ne'er-do-well drifter was apprehended by state
police shortly after the grisly incident, driving a 1962
Plymouth with North Carolina tags. Held on murder and
armed robbery charges. The article related details about the
victim, an off-duty officer with the Barstow PD. It also tagged
Merrick as an ex-Marine with a bad conduct discharge.

Another twenty minutes and she had a birth date, and so armed she dialed up the California State Prison inmate locator service. Five minutes later she located Andy at CSP-Sacramento.

She left a third voice mail for Jack and Ralph.

CHAPTER NINETEEN

Jack's breakfast went down rough, but not because of the food. He was knotted up by the whipsaw from Alex Chung. Jack operated off a playbook, and the walk-off was not in it. Pushing back from the room service table, he tossed the cloth napkin on top of the breakfast remains.

I've got two days, and I'm not wasting one of them contemplating my navel in a hotel room, he thought. He crossed to the window and looked out but hardly saw the scene outside, his mind searching for a productive outlet for his energy. Turning from the still unobserved view, he opened his briefcase and found the sales report Chung had provided.

The print-out sorted customers alphabetically. Starting at the top, Jack searched for Hong Kong based clients. There weren't many. As he paged through slowly a second time, he realized for the first time that most of the affiliate's customers were on the Chinese mainland. Apparently, Quantamica's software was hot in the PRC but not so in Hong Kong or the rest of Asia. He was no expert on Asian sales patterns, but that struck him as odd.

The first local customer he found was BCD Finance— a hundred thousand dollar sale. Developing his line, he dialed their number. On the second ring, a voice answered. "Good morning," Jack replied.

The woman switched to English without missing a beat. "Good morning, sir. How may I assist you?"

"My name is Jack Keane. I'm associated with Quantamica Asia Pacific. I would like to talk to your information systems manager. It's about software BCD recently purchased."

"Just one moment, sir." He listened to music on hold. After thirty seconds, the same voice returned. "I am afraid our systems manager is not available, sir. Can I take your number, and perhaps he can return the call?" Jack provided it.

Bank of South East Asia, Ltd. was the next local client. Jack wasn't confident he could navigate a bank's bureaucracy and reach a knowledgeable someone aware of Quantamica or its software. But he forged ahead. Offering his improvised opening lines, he was initially put on hold for two minutes, then routed to a service manager (sounded like the private banking desk) who seemed confused, went back on hold for another minute, then was transferred back to the same man who fielded his call initially. "I told you so," he said for his own benefit.

In the next hour, he left three more messages. He didn't connect with anyone who recognized the Quantamica name or could talk about its software. It felt like a natural break point for some exercise.

From the hotel, he went right on Nathan Road. After another right towards the harbor, he decided spontaneously to ride the Star Ferry. The trip across to Hong Kong Island took ten minutes. Jack enjoyed the open air and space of the harbor after being cooped in his room. When they reached the ferry pier on the island side, he remained on board for the return trip to Kowloon.

LAST EFFECTS

As they churned back, a memory compartment dormant for years opened—a post card from Daniel, months after he arrived in Vietnam. Mailed from Hong Kong. He couldn't recall the scene on its face, only the message about R&R in Hong Kong, Daniel wanting Jack to know he was thinking of him. Jack recalled asking his father what R&R meant. "Rest and relaxation, son, and I hope your brother is getting both."

Jack Keane made two trips there in the ensuing years, but the card memory hadn't triggered before. Yet another to add to the batch stirred up in the past weeks.

He wasn't clear where things were headed, nor were they as buttoned down as was his norm. The stability of the supposedly immutable past was unsettled, rocked by recent revelations. A new chapter in Daniel's narrative was being written, real time. That instability had carried over to his business, he confessed. The Quantamica engagement had an unfamiliar, discomforting undercurrent, like a game within the game, only he didn't know the rules or how to score.

As unsettling as double jeopardy was to his rational psyche, Jack was convinced both enigmas would be resolved. Perhaps not the neat, tight, all dots connected conclusion he desired, but resolution at least.

He decided to return to the hotel and check messages. Maybe things were progressing faster on the other side of the Pacific.

■   ■   ■   ■

They took the coast highway north from Da Nang. Minh thought they'd make Hue by midday but was less definitive on travel times beyond.

Ralph set three objectives for the trip north with Minh—identify the remnants of the Marine base at Red

LAST EFFECTS

Beach; visit the 1st Amtrak's base camp at Cua Viet; see any special sights along the way, time permitting.

Both men sat in front. The Race was new to the American, part SUV, part van. Minh brought a small kit bag; Ralph's two bags were in back. He'd reconnect with Jack in two days.

They tooled up Highway One. Ralph had been that way before, and as they headed north, he spotted a few familiar landmarks. A temple on the city outskirts, festooned with brightly colored streamers, fit comfortably with his recollection. The traffic—an eclectic mix of pedicabs, motorbikes, cars, light trucks, bicycles, all jockeying for a moment's advantage on the road—was as he remembered, though the vintage of the transport was more recent. Peasants on foot trotted along the shoulder, many carrying heavy loads balanced on shoulder poles.

And there was the smell. The breeze through the open window enveloped Ralph in its distinct bouquet, a memory stimulus. He hadn't a clue to the particular mix of human, industrial, cooking, waste, and animal smells that made it up, but it smelt familiar and nostalgic.

"Marine's there," Minh interrupted Ralph's nasal musing, pointing with his left hand to an imagined perimeter on the opposite side of the highway. What Ralph saw was open space, dotted with a few industrial warehouses. "Base gone," Minh added needlessly, "except buildings," pointing to one of the large warehouses. Villages that bordered the camp had undergone suburban sprawl, encroaching on the confines of Camp Books.

"Minh stop?" he offered.

"No." Gutierrez pointed forward. "Hue."

The driver accelerated, punctuating the Toyota's northward bobbing and weaving with his horn.

LAST EFFECTS

The road began climbing the pass through the mountains that stretch east to west across the countryside to the South China Sea. Ralph's thoughts drifted back to a convoy mission, sometime in 1968. They left Da Nang at dawn, headed to the Marine camp at Phu Bai. The sand-bagged lead truck carried a half dozen Marines and a .50 caliber machine gun mounted above the cab. The barrel swung back and forth in a 180-degree arc as the gunner intently scanned both sides of the road ahead. They were keyed up. The higher they climbed into the pass, the foggier it got. He recalled being spooked as they suddenly lost the morning sun, one moment reflecting brightly on the South China Sea to their right, the next obscured in a fog yet to be burnt off. The driver down-shifted on the switched back road, the multi-fuel engine announcing their arrival with a horrible, grinding protest.

Then a bizarre scene, appropriate only in the unnatural context of a war zone, unfolded. Expecting the blast of a roadside mine or the popping AK-47 fire of an ambush any second, the men hunkered further down in the truck bed. As they rounded another switchback, the driver downshifted again with a loud, double clutching racket. Through the mist, Ralph made out structures on his side of the road—first the base of a concrete wall, then a building, a house, and then out of the fog, a Cinzano umbrella above a table. Gradually, the scene came into focus as they crawled by at five miles per hour—a roadside café, three small tables with chairs, one with the umbrella raised, and a squad of Marines sitting in their combat gear, silently watching the lead truck pass. Ralph felt relief and then a rush of embarrassment.

"What is this called," he asked Minh.

"Hai Van," he replied. "Ocean Clouds."

Perfect, Ralph thought.

CHAPTER TWENTY

Riding up in the hotel elevator, the bellman asked Jack if he needed a Hong Kong tailor. "Do I look like I need one?" he replied good-humoredly.

"Oh, no, sir," came the reply. Jack's mood did not bridge the cultural divide.

Back in his room, he recovered three voice messages from Impact's phone system. First was the message about Walters' return call. Adrenalin flowing, he paused the voice mail retrieval and considered. It was 2:30 A.M. Eastern Standard Time, an aggressive but somewhat attractive time to call Walters. Momentarily, Jack relished putting him off balance, then dismissed the urge. He had to stay cool, get more than he gave, and see what spin the sergeant put on Daniel's death.

Restarting the message queue, he listened to Becky's second and third calls about Merrick. "Bravo!" he exalted to the room. He left the researcher a thank you, copy to Ralph, informing both he'd return the Walters call later that day.

What to do now? he wondered, pacing the room. The call to Florida was at 8:00 P.M. his time, playing off the twelve hour time difference. He considered returning to the customer list when the phone rang.

"Mr. Keane, this is Miss Ng. I have Mr. Chung on the line. May I put him through?"

"Please."

A moment later, the managing director came on. "Mr. Keane, Alex here. I am sorry about today, sir. Please forgive me."

"I hope your emergency is remedied, Alex. Is everything okay?"

"Yes, okay now, thank you. It was a family matter, and unfortunately I am an only son. I had to respond to help my mother. Again, please accept my apology."

"Perhaps we can get together now and pick up our discussion?" Jack groped to rescue part of the day.

"Unfortunately, I am away from Hong Kong, Mr. Keane. I will return tonight. My mother lives on the mainland."

We're batting a thousand here, Jack wanted to say. "Can we talk now, Alex? Or do you need to get off the phone?"

"We can talk for a few minutes, Mr. Keane."

"I contacted customers from the sales report you sent. In five calls, I wasn't able to talk with anyone that ever heard of Quantamica or its software. Customers that already bought our product and owe us money. How do you explain that?"

"Easily, Mr. Keane. They are Chinese, you are not. They do not know you, and we are discrete. Quiet, polite, and discrete. Which customers did you call?"

Jack rattled off the list.

"Not a good use of your time, Mr. Keane, but that is my fault. I will meet you tomorrow for breakfast. Then we will visit Bank of South East Asia. I will introduce you, and they will answer any questions. Is that acceptable, Mr. Keane?"

They agreed to meet at eight-thirty.

"And I suggest you not make any more calls, Mr. Keane."

"I understand, given the reasons you just gave."

"Yes," Chung chimed, "but also many customers on that report have now paid us, so you'll confuse them if you suggest they still owe us money."

Another surprise. Chung sent that list one week before. "How much have you collected in the past week?"

"Almost four million dollars. I have been busy since our first call, asking customers to speed up payments. As I promised, they responded. I will see you at breakfast, Mr. Keane."

For the second time that day, Jack felt he was on the wrong field, equipped for a different game.

CHAPTER TWENTY-ONE

Time to make that call, Jack steeled himself. He ate dinner in his room to make sure he didn't miss any calls. And he didn't.

He dialed international direct access and, after the familiar bong, punched in the Florida number. The telephone cord was short, so he sat on the edge of the bed, facing the small table that held the phone. On the third ring, Walters picked up.

"Yeah?" *This guy has definitely not taken the Dale Carnegie course,* Jack thought.

"Sergeant Walters, Jack Keane."

Walters hesitated. "Hello. It's no longer Sergeant Walters. I retired years ago. Just Eric Walters these days."

"Okay, Mr. Walters. I need to understand how my brother died. I believe you can help."

"It's Jack, right?"

"Yes."

"Well, Jack, that's thirty-five years ago. I'm surprised you're calling me now. I'd like to help, you know, a Marine's next of kin and all. I'm not sure why you're calling all of a sudden?"

"My brother's gear just got back from Vietnam. That reopened things."

"Jack, now I'm really confused. You say his gear was just shipped back from Vietnam? How's that possible? Where was it?"

"Okinawa. His sea bag—the one he left there. It just came home."

Silence.

"Sergeant, you still with me?" Jack probed, returning to the military salutation.

"I'm here. I'm just surprised. Never heard of anything like that. What was in the sea bag?"

Jack tugged on the string. "All sorts of things. I'm calling about how my brother died. I need to hear it from you."

"What can I add that you didn't hear in 1968? I wasn't with your brother when he died, Jack. He was alone. I don't see what else I can tell you."

"What caused his death, sergeant?"

"As I recall, a grenade. A grenade explosion at close range."

"Why did he die? For what reason, sergeant?" Jack deliberately crossed a line, confronting the gruff ex-Marine, poking him with a verbal stick.

"How the hell do I know? He was depressed. You get guys in a combat zone, surround them with weapons, and bad things happen, Jack. I have no idea why your brother killed himself."

"He killed himself?"

"Yes. That's what the investigation said. It may not be what you want to hear, but that's the way it was."

"Sergeant, what were the boys in the band?"

It was as if Jack sent an electrical charge through the phone—he could sense shock at the other end.

"Who were the what?" Walters finally muttered.

"The boys in the band. What were they?"

"I have no flipping idea who they were!"

"I didn't ask who they were, sergeant. What were they? But now that you've asked, who were they? Some of your team at Red Beach?"

"I told you, I have no idea what the boys in the band is. . . or was. Now listen, Keane, I tried to help, but I've told you all I can. I'm sorry he died, but I don't see how else I can help. And I need to hang up. I have an appointment."

"Sure, sergeant. Do you get *Leatherneck*?"

"Yeah. Why?"

"Take a look at the last issue. I put out feelers and I got a response. I'll share it with you when I'm back."

"What was it?" But the connection dropped midway through his question, as Jack hung up.

Eric Walters put the receiver down and walked to the magazine rack by his chair. Paging through it, he found *Mail Call*. He skimmed down, spotting the bold typed name three quarters down the page.

■   ■   ■   ■

"Becky, copy for Ralph. Thanks for the follow through on Merrick. Here's an update and a request." Jack paused for a moment, catching his breath.

"Connected with Walters this morning your time. Conversation rattled him. I bushwhacked him with Daniel's gear just arriving, and his anxiety heightened from that point on. The 'boys in the band' got his adrenalin flowing, but he denied knowing anything. Then I told him we have a response from Mail Call. Let's let him stew in that for a bit. Our next conversation with him has to be face to face.

"Becky, set us up for a meeting with Andy Merrick at CSP-Sacramento. Book Ralph and me through San Francisco on our return.

"Next to last, develop all you can on Walters. Assets, credit bureaus, employment history, the works. Need to know what asset base he's accumulated. You know where I'm going—the money trail, as best you can develop it. Call your buddies at the IRS and find out how to get them interested, assuming you turn up what I suspect.

"Final point, unrelated to earlier. Call Ephraim for me. Tell him there's an interesting development in Hong Kong. Have him call our client and quietly get up to speed on the ownership structure of their affiliate here. I need to know how much is owned by Rock Creek, by others, and who those others are. We'll discuss next week."

■　　■　　■　　■

Minh deferred to Ralph on spending the night in Quang Tri or Dong Ha. Both were a short distance to their ultimate destination, Cua Viet. Ralph's initial instinct was to call it a day in Quang Tri, but impulsively, as Minh slowed after entering the provincial capital, Ralph pointed forward, mouthing "Dong Ha." Nonplussed, the Vietnamese put the car into third gear and accelerated north.

Quang Tri was headquarters of the 3rd Marine Division during Ralph's tour. He reported at the heavily sandbagged division headquarters bunker one night in 1968, armed with an M-16 and orders to join the 1st Amphibious Tractor Battalion. "They're out at the mouth of the Cua Viet," the master sergeant informed him. "Pitch your gear in one of the headquarters area huts for tonight, sergeant, and then catch a chopper or Mike boat up there in the morning."

A more vivid memory was three hours earlier that day, on the Dong Ha airstrip. He hitched a ride on a C-130 transport for the flight from Da Nang up to the DMZ with a dozen other Marines and a hold filled with palletized supplies. As the plane approached Dong Ha, the crew chief addressed them over the roar of the four turboprops. "When we hit the landing strip," he yelled, "the pilot's going to slow this baby down real quick to about ten miles an hour. Grab your gear, whatever you can carry, and roll off the ramp while we're still moving, because we ain't gonna stop. There's slit trenches on both sides. Haul ass and stay down, because we'll take incoming, count on that. Wait five minutes before you come out to pick up the rest of your gear."

Initially he was skeptical, suspecting the chief was indulging in some new guy hazing at his expense. Immediately after the speech, however, the C-130 nosed suddenly towards the corrugated steel strips laid end to end to form the runway. Ralph bounced along with the plane as its wheels touched down at speed, heard the roar of the propellers reversing to slow the snub-nosed transport, and felt the pilot brake hard. The men rocked forward with the sudden deceleration, then popped back upright, finally stood and began wobbling to the rear of the aircraft. The crew chief already had the tail ramp down, and as the plane slowed, he hurried them along. "Come on, come on, get down here. Here we go!" he shouted. Then they were tumbling individually off the ramp, each with rifle in hand, rolling as they hit the ground, scrambling crab-legged toward the safety of the slit trenches. As promised, he heard incoming rounds, the NVA trying to catch them in the open, perhaps even score a lucky kill on the transport. Never stopping, the plane pivoted at the end of the steel runway and roared back the way it came.

He decided they'd stay in Dong Ha tonight. He had no idea what accommodations were available, but he wasn't worried. They'd find something. "Dong Ha," he repeated.

Half an hour later they rolled into town. Minh worked both sides of the main strip with his eyes, looking for a place to stay. He turned left, braking in front of a small hotel. Looking at the sign, Ralph turned to the already smiling Minh.

Ralph laughed. He and Minh grabbed their overnight kits and entered the Dong Ha Hotel.

■　　　■　　　■　　　■

Jack sat next to Chung as their taxi left the Kowloon Hotel. The managing director gave the driver rapid instructions, Jack assuming that Bank of South East Asia was embedded in the word stream.

"When is your departure flight?" Alex inquired.

"Four this afternoon, so I'll leave for the airport by two."

"I didn't realize there was a flight to the States that time of the afternoon. What airline are you flying?"

"Vietnam Air. To Da Nang."

Chung turned to face Jack on the bench seat. "You have business in Vietnam, Mr. Keane?"

"No, it's personal. I'm meeting an associate."

"Vietnam is attracting more tourists and investment. An economic tiger in the making, do you think?" He smiled.

Jack didn't have an opinion.

"But they are difficult people to do business with. Communists are still in charge, even though they put on a capitalist face to attract investment. Too many hands in other people's pockets," Alex chuckled.

"Unlike the People's Republic?" Jack's offhand had intent.

"Not at all," Chung rebutted. "China is a much better country to do business in, much less corrupt. There is no comparison, Mr. Keane."

"My apologies. I meant no offense." *But I did hit a nerve.*

"No offense taken." The rest of the ride passed in silence.

Five minutes later they pulled up to one of the steel and glass towers that punctuate the Kowloon landscape. Chung led the way, ushering Jack to the elevator bank, and pressed the button for fourteen. They exited onto a wide, carpeted hallway, turned right, and stopped at glass double doors with Bank of South East Asia, Ltd. stenciled across.

After presenting themselves to the receptionist, Alex handling the introductions, they were led to a conference room along the exterior wall. The wealth of glass afforded a panoramic view of the harbor and Hong Kong.

Mr. Ko, introduced as the bank's information systems manager, joined them. He and Jack shook hands and swapped business cards. After the bank manager politely studied Keane's card, the three men took seats around the conference table. Some casual talk preceded Alex's context setter for the meeting.

"Mr. Keane is consulting with Quantamica's American affiliate. They are pleased with our success in Asia, and he is here to meet with a few important customers, to understand our success better. We appreciate your time in meeting with us." Both heads turned to Jack.

After seconding Chung's thank you, Jack moved onto more interesting terrain. "I'm interested in how you use Quantamica's software and how the installation and support has progressed. And to see if you have any problems or suggestions for us." He stopped, giving Ko broad entrée to take the conversation wherever he pleased.

"Thank you, Mr. Keane. I am pleased to share our experiences. It is gratifying that your investors are interested in our opinion." Ko reported the bank ordered Quantamica's pattern recognition software tool, *Fraudent*, eight months before. Jack knew such software took a few months to stabilize to operate effectively. It had to learn what to look for. Fraudent was brilliant at spotting unusual events while rapidly culling through millions of transactions—a New York issued credit card suddenly generating a twenty-five dollar gas station charge on the U.S.-Mexico border, or a first time purchase at an inner city jewelry store. He listened as the systems manager related their experience.

Per Ko, installation was routine, begun once the bank's home office approved the purchase. Installation, the first step, took a month, which in Jack's experience was fast. Optimizing, Fraudent learning to spot dubious transactions, came next. That typically took a few months, Jack recalled, as the software was exposed to large volumes of transactions. But in the bank's case, the software was optimized in a scant thirty days. *These guys must be good,* he thought. Then they went live and were operational the last five months. "We are very satisfied, Mr. Keane," the manager wound up his testimonial.

"Were there installation problems that were not resolved to your satisfaction?" Ko indicated none. "So Fraudent has been performing well for"—Jack paused a moment—"five months?"

"Yes, that is correct." Ko smiled.

"Can I ask why the bank took so long to pay?"

"I understood from Mr. Chung that was your concern. You know the bank has now paid?" His eyebrows rose.

"Yes. So I was told."

"By bank transfer last week," Ko added gratuitously.

"Thank you. But again, why the delay?"

Ko seemed a trifle surprised at being pressed. It was obvious to Jack the two men had rehearsed his visit beforehand. Apparently they were in unscripted territory.

"It had nothing to do with the product. It was an internal issue. South East Asia Bank is a young company, and it took us time to get the payment authorized." The bank manager offered that as if obvious that all was now well, neatly explained, tied up in a conversational bow, pushed across the table to his guest.

So the slow pay issue was simply the result of bank red tape? Jack looked to Chung for confirmation, but the managing director was busy with his digital assistant, missing or uninterested in the exchange.

Apparently, there was nothing else to learn. To move the conversation, Jack asked a final question. "What is Fraudent monitoring?"

"Credit and debit card transactions."

As expected. That was Fraudent's bread and butter utility, reducing bogus transactions and saving millions in fraud prevention. Jack kept the conversational ball moving as he waited for Chung to tune back in. "How many cards has the bank issued, Mr. Ko?" The minimum number of active accounts that justified an expensive tool like Fraudent was a million. Anything less meant the issuer couldn't justify it with expected savings.

"Not many, Mr. Keane. We are in the process of building our customer base."

Jack kept a straight face, but that was nonsense. Why lay out cash today for a product that would practically sit on the shelf while they built a use for it? Either they were naive, inept, or Chung and his team were selling ice to the Eskimos.

He glanced over at Chung again, but the local director had either missed the moment or, worse still, didn't comprehend its significance. He dropped the line of inquiry. *Save this for later.*

"I appreciate your time, Mr. Ko. For my information, what payment did the bank make?"

"$550,000, Mr. Keane."

Jack exercised the same facial control muscles for the second time to keep his jaw from bouncing off the table. He wanted to shriek, *What?* Shell out over half a million for a product that won't pay back savings until you have millions of transactions? What was going on? The bank manager still wore his pleasant smile.

"Bank of South East Asia is just starting up?"

"Yes. We are expanding quickly."

"And it's a PRC organized company?" Jack guessed.

"That is correct." Ko asked if there was anything else he could offer? Did they need a car called?

Seeing Ko rising from his seat, signaling an end to the interview, Chung tuned back in. Jack stood for a moment with the bank manager, shaking hands. "Is the bank publicly traded?" he asked Ko.

"No. Privately owned."

"And who is the owner?"

"That I cannot help you with," Ko responded. "I am a systems manager, Mr. Keane, not investor relations."

Chung held the door for Jack.

CHAPTER TWENTY-TWO

Jack arrived at the Da Nang Hotel just after 9:00 P.M. "Is Mr. Gutierrez checked in?" he asked at the desk.

"No, sir. But he is expected."

He left a message for Ralph to ring him, then found his third floor room.

He and Chung had spent another hour together after the bank visit. In a meeting at Quantamica's Kowloon office, Alex provided a current customer report, including amounts now owed after the recent collections success. "This is up-to-date as of yesterday, close of business," he volunteered. "The payment situation is much improved."

Jack asked a few questions, selecting individual clients and lobbing in one or two follow-up queries on each, but it was form over substance. He knew he was being fed a story and had tired of the stage show. It was easy to expose the holes in the bank's story, but what was the real game? How did the $550,000 charade fit into a bigger picture? He recalled a trial lawyer once pontificating, "Never ask a question in court unless you already know the answer." That didn't work in consulting, but the caution felt right just then.

Looking at his watch, he suggested it was time to return to his hotel, pack and head to the airport.

Chung offered to accompany him, but Jack said that was unnecessary. As they parted on the street, Alex hailed a taxi. "I hope all your questions have been answered, Mr. Keane."

"It's been interesting. I don't know what else to ask."

■   ■   ■   ■

It was after eleven when the phone rang in Jack's room.

"Up for a drink?"

"Sounds good. In the bar, five minutes," Jack suggested.

Ralph sat at a table, accompanied by two tumblers with Scotch and ice. He rose from the chair to greet Jack.

The men studied each other as they enjoyed their drinks. Jack looked tired and a bit unsettled. Keane was on unfamiliar turf, Ralph surmised, used to more control. For the first time, the Marine considered the impact of no firm resolution to their effort. He'd go on to something new, but Jack would carry that ambiguity forward.

To Jack, Ralph seemed his most at ease in their short relationship. He was on familiar turf, Jack reflected. As career military, much of his life was lived outside the United States, a fair amount in the Third World. Being a stranger in a strange land was business as usual for Gutierrez. He envied Ralph's comfort.

"How did it go in Hong Kong?"

"Good and bad. The good part, the local guy has supposedly done a gangbuster job collecting cash from customers. So one of the major problems they were wrestling with is fixed." Jack took another pull at the whiskey. "On the flip side, something a lot more complicated than slow pay is going on. Not sure what, but it isn't what they claim."

"What might explain what you saw, Jack? Can you unpack and reassemble the pieces so it does make sense?"

"Yeah, but that's not my long suit, Ralph. I've come across fraud before, but the garden variety kind—cooking the books, phony vendors, sham contracts—that kind of thing. I've never seen an instance where the business itself was the sham, a front to avoid scrutiny. The fraud I've encountered before was a business byproduct—never the main event."

Ralph had nothing else to offer. He appreciated the "double whammy" to Jack, dealing with the implied fraud of his brother's death while fighting on a second front with Quantamica. A lot to carry. He didn't know how to say that without sounding patronizing.

"How was your trip north?"

"Great." Ralph was surprised at his spontaneous word choice. "Found a decent guide. Saw everything I wanted. Thanks for the flex to take a couple of days private time."

"I'm glad it was useful. Let's talk about tomorrow."

They turned to their game plan. Ralph had retained Minh for at least one more day and now suggested their itinerary, based on his drive by of Red Beach. They agreed to meet for breakfast at eight and left the bar together.

Jack's sleep that night was disturbed by an atypical nightmare. He was in the passenger seat of a speeding car, Alex Chung at the wheel. Instead of focusing on the road ahead, Chung was facing him, smiling, telling him not to worry. Jack could see a fork approaching, but when he looked back, Daniel was now at the wheel. His brother was asking a question, but Jack couldn't quite hear the words above the whine of the engine. "Which way?" he finally made out.

He awoke in a sweat.

■   ■   ■   ■

Eric Walters collected his mail at the Jacksonville Beach post office, box 453. His routine was to pass through on his daily walk, then return to the beach, incorporating a pit stop and coffee break along the way.

He deposited his mail on one of the waist high sorting tables that faced the windows looking out on Route A1A. Junk mail went to the trash bin, magazines and periodicals to the bottom of the stack, regular mail on top. After a quick scan of the return addresses on the first class mail, everything was tucked under his left arm for the brisk return journey. He'd open interesting items over coffee.

As instructed, he posted a note to the Colonel after connecting with Keane. The revelation of the sea bag's arrival and *Leatherneck* trolling exercise unsettled him, but he was cautiously optimistic that Keane had nowhere to go, at least nowhere in the direction of Eric Walters. He followed orders, and Evans ordered him to send that note after he made contact. Though aging rapidly, the old man was still formidable, and Walters had no intention of getting offside with him or the other "boys." He didn't know how Evans and his friends might deal with insubordination, and he had no desire to find out.

He sat down at one of the small, wrought iron tables outside the coffee shop and emptied the carrying tray of his coffee and carrot and bran muffin. The mail sat at table center. Scanning the letters, he noticed one from the company he used to protect against identity theft. Opening it first, he expected a routine "no activity." He had no need for credit and used plastic only for convenience. No mortgage, no car payment, no gas cards, he lived debt free.

The privacy update reported a credit inquiry on him. He didn't recognize the name. More important, he hadn't asked for a loan or anything else that warranted a credit check. It was a snoop. And he knew who was driving it.

His face hardened, he rose from the table, leaving the rest of his coffee and muffin.

■   ■   ■   ■

Minh was in the lobby when they emerged from breakfast, marking time next to a potted plant, unobtrusively attired in white short-sleeved shirt, black pants and rubber soled shoes. Ralph made the introductions, Minh inclining his head as he shook Jack's hand.

The plan for the day was agreed. First up was Camp Books. Jack knew the base was long gone but still wanted to see the place. A second objective, albeit a long shot, was to circulate through the villages in the immediate environs of Red Beach, showing the picture of Daniel with the young Vietnamese girl when the opportunity presented.

Jack brought copies of all the album photos. As they prepared to pull away from the hotel, Ralph handed them to Minh with instructions. "Take a look. We're interested in anything in those photos, as well as the villages close to the old Marine base. Okay?"

Minh nodded, thumbing through the photocopied pages, sixteen pictures in all. "That is your brother?" he asked Jack, holding up the page with the photo of Daniel and the girl.

"Yes. His name was Daniel."

"Who is girl?"

"Don't know," Jack answered, "but someone around the base might." Minh didn't look optimistic as he nodded his understanding.

"Two villages," Minh volunteered. "Da Phuc, Hoa Khahn. After base?"

"After base," Jack agreed.

"We pass on way," Minh said, pointing to the photo they assumed was a temple.

■ ■ ■ ■

Three hours later, they had finished touring the remnants of Camp Books. They ended where they had started, in front of one of the three large, steel framed, concrete floored structures which occupied a triangle of sand in the northwest corner of the former camp. The buildings now housed light industry—a metalworking and machine shop, maintenance garage and a warehouse.

When they first arrived, Minh used his supply of Marlboros liberally, finally striking up a conversation with one of the older men working in the machine shop. While he enjoyed the cigarette, Mr. Nhu explained he had worked there for many years. During the war, he did metal work as part of the support operations at the base. "Americans good to work for," Nhu continued through Minh's translation. "Good tools, nice people, but too much waste."

Minh suggested Nhu give them a walking tour, and the old man agreed. The four walked the sandy confines, Nhu at times pointing to supplement his oral history. At the start, they showed Nhu the photos. Some scenes he recognized, including the snapshot of Marines in front of what looked like a mess hall or club (it was both, per Nhu). He didn't recognize Keane or the girl.

The combination mess hall and club stood in the center of the base, Nhu explained, pointing to a concrete slab on their left. The structure was cannibalized after the war, corrugated steel sheets converted to roof tops and walls in the surrounding villages. Off to their right, Nhu pointing out, were living quarters. It was now vacant sand, picked clean over the years of any remnants of the wooden, canvas, and sandbag village within the camp.

As they walked east, Mr. Nhu pointed out the former landing zone. A hundred yards ahead, the north-south Highway One carried its traffic. "Entrance here," Minh pointed directly in front of them, mimicking Nhu. "Vietnamese come through gate here to work." Nhu looked around, as if seeing things as they were then. "Barbed wire all around base, bunkers, machine guns, trip flares," he rattled on in Vietnamese, Minh translating with a few seconds delay. The elderly eyes swept the four points of the rectangle of the Marine logistics campus, describing it as it was then.

Jack conjured up a mental image of what had been from the collage of Daniel's photos, Nhu's words and his own imagination. The place was his brother's home for one of his nineteen years. Little remained—occasional sandbag remnants, the concrete slab of the formless mess hall. If he raked through the sand, he guessed he'd find other detritus from Daniel's time—shell casings, C-ration containers, human waste, all part of the site's archeology. The most sensitive instruments, he supposed, might find traces of his brother's DNA in the earth.

"Let's visit those villages," Jack suggested, after they walked the full perimeter and much of the interior of the compound. They turned back toward the Toyota. When they reached the metal shop, Jack handed Nhu a ten dollar bill, thanking him for his assistance. The old man smiled, enfolding Jack's hand within both his leathery paws. He said some words, keeping hold of the right hand, a sincere look on his face. Then he turned and shook Ralph's hand and finally Minh's.

Minh didn't translate immediately. After he started the car and was pulling away, Jack asked about the parting words. "He also lose brother in war. But he never able to bury his brother. He say your brother's spirit no longer in Vietnam. It go home with his body."

CHAPTER TWENTY-THREE

Seated at a circular table, the three men picked at the chicken, rice and vegetables before them. The restaurant, a converted barge, rode peacefully at its moorings on the Da Nang River.

Minh selected the place. They agreed on an early dinner, given no lunch and dry throats. The first bottles of beer were dispatched quickly, their seconds supplementing the food. Table conversation was sparse as they ate, not from any awkwardness between them, more an indication of their hunger and mutual comfort. They didn't need to fill empty spaces with chatter, content with silent stretches interspersed with bursts of dialogue.

■   ■   ■   ■

After leaving the base, they drove to Hoa Khahn, bordering Red Beach on its southern perimeter. The village straddled the highway, its center on the west side of the road. Minh pulled off onto an unpaved side road and drove inland a short distance before stopping. He got out of the car and approached two old women sitting hunched in front of a wood and tin structure, one of many look-a-likes in that area. After Minh offered cigarettes, their conversation yielded fruit, one of the women pointing. Minh showed them the photo page, pointing to the young girl, but both heads shook no.

Returning, he reported the women suggested they visit Mr. Hahn, a village elder. "We walk," he indicated. After further words with the two, he handed each another cigarette. "We leave car."

They followed Minh down the road one hundred yards, then cut right down a thin dirt path that meandered through the motley housing. Minh asked directions twice more before they found Hahn's house. The two Americans held back while the driver walked to the corrugated metal overhang of the porch, then introduced himself through the screen door. A voice responded, Minh and his interlocutor engaging in a short dialogue. He turned to his companions and beckoned them forward as he opened the screen door. "Should we leave our shoes outside?" Jack asked before entering.

"Not necessary," Minh replied. "Old man say come in. His daughter not home, he not feeling well, but okay enough to see us." It was dark inside, the only light provided by two small windows, one on each side wall of what looked like a sitting room. Ralph assumed that a closed door in the rear wall connected to a further room, since there was no window. A small lamp with an incongruous Tiffany style shade sat on a table next to Mr. Hahn's chair. The old man remained seated as they entered. Minh, inclining the top half of his body toward Hahn, introduced the visitors. Smiling, the old man pointed to the two additional chairs that occupied corners of the small room. He said something to Minh while pointing to the door behind him. The driver went through it and returned with a small hard backed chair, which he set to the left of Hahn and sat down.

An offer of tea followed, which Minh translated and suggested he'd decline politely, since the daughter was not home and, if they accepted, a neighbor would have to come in to provide the hospitality. Then followed statements by Minh, questions from Hahn, answers from Minh, all interspersed with looks from Hahn to Jack and, less frequently, Ralph. Finally, their driver rose and showed the photo sheets, the girl photo on top. Squinting in the light, Hahn indicated he didn't recognize her. But he held onto all the sheets, looking closely at the other images on the top page. Minh extended his hand for the pages, but Hahn instead flipped to the second page. Working his way down the images, he pointed with pinky finger at one, a group of Marines standing in front of a warehouse. He said something to Minh, pointing again at the photo. The ping-pong of question, reply, follow up question and response repeated three times. Finally, Jack asked Minh what the exchange was about.

"Mr. Hahn not know girl, but he say that picture familiar. That man they call Ham."

Ralph got up and looked at the picture the elder was fingering. "I don't recall anyone named Ham on the roster," he said to Jack over Hahn's shoulder.

On hearing that, Minh intervened. "No, Ham is name Vietnamese call him, not American name. Ham mean greedy. This Marine called Greedy."

"Why was he called Greedy?" Jack asked.

Minh to Hahn, Hahn to Minh, Minh to the two Americans. "He not honest. With Americans. Not with Vietnamese. Always cheat."

"How did he cheat Americans?" Jack asked. Hahn laughed when that was translated and launched into an animated response, words pouring forth, enjoying the opportunity to share an anecdote. Minh started translating in progress.

"He use Vietnamese all the time to load trucks, load helicopters, that then drive away, take off. All quick, quick, load boxes, close doors, go away." Minh paused, then picked up the continuous translation again. "Greedy even have whiskey, beer, Coca Cola delivered to Da Nang for night clubs, take back piasters, dollars. But he always cheat Vietnamese." Then almost as an afterthought, he added, "And Americans. He steal from his own people."

As they left, Jack asked how they could thank Mr. Hahn without insulting him. Minh suggested a cash gift, acknowledging that a village elder needs money to help his people. Jack laid twenty dollars in Hahn's hand while Minh conveyed the sentiment. The elder seemed surprised, then grateful, then touched, all expressed in a fluid recasting of his features. He and Jack shook hands.

■　　■　　■　　■

"What's the plan for tomorrow," Ralph asked Jack as they finished dinner. "Any other places you want to see?"

"No, I don't think so—not optimistic there's any more for me here, and I'm not up for sightseeing. I'm going to try to move my departure forward to tomorrow. I want to get to California and meet Merrick."

Ralph wasn't surprised. He agreed with Jack's assessment and plan.

Minh took them to the hotel, and waited in the bar with Ralph while Jack tested the art of the possible on itinerary changes through the concierge. Thirty minutes later, he joined them. "We take a ten o'clock flight tomorrow morning. We'll connect in Taipei for the San Francisco leg."

LAST EFFECTS

Ralph offered to settle up for the last three days, but Minh insisted he take them to the airport. "I be here at eight," Minh suggested. "Goodnight, friends."

■　　■　　■　　■

Becky located John Lettman, former Luitenant, USMC, at his office in Arlington, Virginia. Mrs. Lettman was comfortable providing his work number, once she understood the call pertained to Marine Corps business. Her husband was proud of his service, had stayed in the reserves after his active duty tour, and she knew he would assist a dead Marine's next of kin in any way possible.

Compared to the other priority targets, Lettman had been a breeze. He kept his contact details current in the Marine Reserve Officer's Association, and Becky received a response to her initial message within a day.

Now dialing his work number, Lettman picked up on the second ring. Becky introduced herself, then started into the same background paragraph she used earlier. But after the first sentence, he interrupted. "Ms. Wolfe, my wife already told me about your call. I understand it's about a deceased Marine. How can I help?"

She used their standard script, the possible appeal to have a Vietnam Marine's name added to the War Memorial.

"What's the man's name?"

"Corporal Daniel Keane."

"I don't recall him, Ms. Wolfe. What outfit was he with?"

"Force Logistics Command." Becky suggested her employer, Jack Keane, the brother, share the details.

"Sure. Have him call me." But Lettman's voice had lost some life, Becky noted.

CHAPTER TWENTY-FOUR

California State Prison-Sacramento. "Hard to miss, even if you weren't looking for it," Ralph cracked, making a right off Folsom Boulevard into the prison parking lot.

They arrived in San Francisco the night before after twenty-four hours of travel. Refreshed after an overnight at the Fairmont, they were in a rental car by nine for the two hour drive northeast to Represa, home of both Folsom and CSP-Sacramento.

Becky's advance work had secured them a two-on-one meeting, Jack and Ralph with Merrick. Not a typical prison visit, yet Becky managed to get it approved, including use of a private meeting room usually reserved for client-attorney sessions.

After presenting photo ID in duplicate, then passing two security screens, Ralph and Jack were escorted to meeting room four. The room itself had floor to ceiling glass on three sides, giving security full view of the occupants. Their escort indicated chairs on the far side of the conference table. "The inmate sits here, closest to the door," she pointed. "You're not to give the prisoner anything—no cigarettes, food, gifts, money. Deposit anything you want him to have with security. They'll deliver it after it's been screened. Any questions?"

"Two," Jack answered. "I want to show Merrick some photos. Is that allowed?"

"Let's see." After reviewing them, she laid the three sheets on the table next to the empty chair.

"We may need to take notes. Any problem with that?"

"No. Just don't give him anything."

A minute later, Andy Merrick was escorted in. He wore a plain gray top, same shade gray trousers, white socks, black shoes. Short hair, gray with dark patches, balding top, thin face, horn-rim glasses, prominent ears. Ralph thought Merrick looked more like the Maytag repairman than a lifer for homicide. The escort motioned Merrick into the vacant chair, consulted his watch, and said he'd return in thirty minutes.

Jack realized he hadn't asked if they were allowed to shake hands. Remaining seated, he extended his hand across the table. "Mr. Merrick, my name's Jack Keane. This is Ralph Gutierrez. Thanks for meeting with us."

Andy took the proffered hand, nodding to Jack and then Ralph.

Jack continued. "Thanks for answering my Mail Call. Daniel was my older brother. I'm trying to find out how he died. Mr. Gutierrez is helping me."

Andy turned to Ralph. "Are you a private detective?"

"No."

"Retired cop?"

"No. I'm a Marine."

"I would have guessed. In time. That squared away look. The alignment. You know it when you see it."

Turning back to Jack, "How can I help you, Mr. Keane?"

"It's Jack. Mind if I call you Andy?"

"Not at all."

"I'd like to hear about my brother. How he lived, how he died." They had agreed beforehand that Jack would take the lead. Ralph would take notes and watch for non-verbal cues.

"Well, like I said in my letter, I didn't know your brother real well. He seemed like a decent guy. Always treated me with respect. But we didn't run in the same pack. He was in-country a good six months before I got to 'Nam. I was warehouse crew, operated a fork lift, loading supplies, stuff like that, but your brother worked in the office. He was squared away, but I was more of a . . . " he paused, "more of a screw up."

"Did you two have a lot of contact?"

"Not too much. We used to shape up once a week for inspection. Gunny Walters liked to go through the motions of some close order drill, weapons inspection, that sort of thing. And your brother was out in the warehouse sometimes, checking on things. I'd see him at chow, but we didn't sit together. He'd come out to the warehouse and get a Coke. We kept a reefer, a refrigerator, in the main warehouse."

Jack paused, giving Merrick time to complete his answers. "Did he hang out with any of the other men? Any buddies?"

"Yeah, he had one or two guys that he hung with, but not all the time. They were in-country for a while; sort of old salts, but not in an arrogant way. You typically ran with the guys you rotated in with. It wasn't so much that they were different, they just didn't hang out as much in the club as we did. Not as much drinking and grab assing, if you know what I mean. More squared away, gung ho."

"Gung ho?"

Andy pushed his chair back a bit, thinking. "Like, for instance, your brother volunteered for stuff. Patrols, perimeter duty, convoys, that sort of thing. I remember once,

Walters needed volunteers for a convoy run. Your brother practically begged to go. I asked him, how come? What did he know? Was it an easy gig? He smiled, said no, not as far as he knew, but it could be an adventure, and at least it was different. Then he asked me why didn't I come along? That surprised me. I didn't think he had any time for me. But I passed." Merrick looked wistful for a moment, like he wished he'd said yes.

"How did my brother get along with the other men?"

"Okay. Live and let live. Nobody went out of their way to piss someone off, you know. You stayed with your clique. But Daniel seemed to treat just about everybody with respect."

"Just about everybody?"

Andy reflected. The delay was more than simply pausing to frame an answer. Merrick was making a choice, Jack speculated, about where he was going to take the interview. *Why tell the truth, if a lie will suffice?* Jack thought. Certainly Merrick had developed a facility for lying.

Apparently resolved, he continued. "Well, your brother was no suck up. And Gunny Walters, he liked things his way. Sometimes, especially after he came back from Okinawa, your brother and the Gunny would get pretty tense with each other."

"Why?"

"Your brother was by the book. The Gunny was looser, around supplies and paperwork, that is. They had a few discussions about missing supplies, paperwork—a pallet of refrigerators gone missing, that sort of thing. And then there was the clubs warehouse fiasco."

That was new. Ralph made a note. "What's that about?" Jack prodded.

Andy looked up at the corner where the glass wall met the ceiling, pulling up the memory. "When it happened, I thought it was comical. Funny how perspective changes with time. The clubs warehouse was right behind us. Beer, booze, slots, everything was there. Right behind us! Walters was tight with the sergeant who ran it. I forget his name. Anyway, one day, pure daylight, a Chinook lands next to the warehouse. Not on the LZ. No, the pilot sets it down in the road right there. Sand flying everywhere! And the Gunny tells two of us to go over and help load the bird up. Cases of Scotch, whiskey, top shelf stuff. We filled it. And then off it goes."

"What happened then?"

"Well, your brother came looking for a crew and none of us were around. He came around the building, saw what was going on, and asks me what the hell were we doing? I said ask the Gunny, and he heads off, looking for Walters. And he found him. When we finished, we went into the warehouse to stash our gifts, a fifth each. Your brother and Walters were in the warehouse, the Gunny telling him to stick to his requisitions, mind his own f'ing business, or the Gunny would fix his ass good."

Jack absorbed that. After a few seconds, he asked, "Andy, who were the boys in the band?"

The animated expression that accompanied the helicopter episode disappeared. In a flat voice, Merrick replied, "I don't know."

"Ever heard the expression before?"

"No," said with his head down.

Another pause. "You found Daniel's body?"

Andy nodded.

"Tell me about it."

"It wasn't pretty. Your brother was dead a while."

"Where was he?" Jack leaned forward, arms on the table.

"In one of the small bunkers in the warehouse area—a 'just in case' bunker."

"Just in case?"

"Just in case we took incoming, and needed a hole to crawl into." Andy looked up, smiling at the memory.

"Why was he there?" Jack's voice had an edge.

"Not that unusual, at least for your brother. It was pretty noisy in our hut. There were ten of us, lot of drinking, carrying on. Sometimes your brother would grab his stuff and sleep out in the bunker. Said it gave him some space, privacy, when he needed it."

"He said that to you?"

"Yes." Andy's head went down again.

"Interesting, given you weren't that close."

"Yeah, I guess so."

"Was noise the only reason he wanted privacy?"

The convict faced Jack. "Don't know. Took him at his word."

Jack eased off, taking his arms off the table. "Was it drugs? Did my brother have a problem?"

"I don't think so." No eye contact.

"You said it might be drugs in your statement."

"You saw that?" Merrick directed to Jack, then looked at Ralph.

"I did. You also said he seemed depressed. That drugs may have been involved."

"Yeah, that's right. I said that, but I don't believe it." His voice was devoid of emotion.

"Why did you say it?"

"The Gunny and I talked. After I found Daniel. He said that your brother was depressed. He knew the signs. With the way he was acting, he was probably doing drugs; erratic, temperamental..."

"So you included that in your statement?"

"Yeah. I figured Walters knew what he was talking about."

"Did Walters ask you to say that?"

"No. Not exactly. He just suggested that was why Daniel blew himself up."

Jack thought about where to take the dialogue. "Why did you go looking for him that morning, Andy? You and Daniel weren't that close."

"When your brother didn't show for duty, Walters sent me to find him."

"Did you check the hut first?"

The head shook no, words followed. "No, I knew he wasn't there. I just left there when I ran into Walters. So the first place I checked was the bunker, and there he was."

"Anybody else around?"

"No." After a pause, "No one but Daniel."

"Do you think my brother killed himself, Andy?"

"I used to. But being inside all these years, I've thought about things. Turned stuff over and over in my mind, look at it from different angles. No, I don't think he purposely killed himself."

"As you've turned things over, who comes to mind when you think about how he died?"

"No one. I just have trouble believing he meant to kill himself."

That didn't ring true. Jack knew without looking that Ralph heard the same false note. He let it lie for now.

"Andy, I don't believe Daniel took his own life." Jack paused half a minute. "Anything else that we should know?"

"No."

Jack straightened in his chair. "Let's switch gears. Can you look through those pictures?" He pointed to the papers on Andy's right. "Tell us if you see anything familiar."

Merrick stared at the top page, the highway shots, village scenes along the road. "Looks like stuff right outside Red Beach." Turning to page two, "There's Hua," his finger pointing. "That one is in front of the main warehouse," Andy said, holding up the page, pointing to the shot of Daniel with three Marines.

"Who's Hua?" Jack asked.

"The girl with your brother."

"How do you know her?"

"She worked in the clubs warehouse."

"Were she and Daniel close?"

"Not like that, I don't think. They were friendly. She taught him some Vietnamese."

"Any way she could have been involved with Daniel's death?"

"No way. She was harmless. All the guys probably had a picture with her."

"Who's in front of the warehouse?"

"One guy's Myerson, I think. There's Gunny Walters. Don't know the other guy."

"Which one is Walters?" Jack asked.

"That one." Merrick pointed to Hahn's *Greedy*.

CHAPTER TWENTY-FIVE

Jack used Sunday to get acclimated to Eastern Standard Time. Supposedly, each hour of time zone change required one day for adjustment. He didn't have that much time, and needed to be fresh Monday, first thing.

He was eating take out from Café Monti, his favorite in town restaurant. The phone rang.

"Mr. Keane, Alex Chung here. Good evening."

Jack wished he had let the call flow to messages. "Good morning, Alex." It was 7:00 P.M. Jack's time, which meant Alex was up early.

"I hope you had a good trip to Vietnam?"

Jack said it was fine.

"I called to discuss a consulting opportunity that has arisen. I believe you will find it of interest." Chung went on to relate that one of his customers needed a high powered American consultant to give them advice on business improvement. They proposed a retainer agreement, Jack committing to give them up to twenty days of his time over the next twelve months.

"They propose a retainer of $100,000, Mr. Keane. Plus, of course, your regular billing for any time and expenses."

Jack thanked Alex for the offer, stating that he would have to get back to him.

They're upping the ante, he thought, disconnecting.

■　　■　　■　　■

He arrived at the Tysons office at 8:10 Monday morning, feeling fresh. After checking voice and e-mail, he looked through the red action file that Becky had centered on his desk. At 8:30, he dialed the Arlington number she provided.

"Lettman."

Jack launched into his introduction to the former CID officer, but was cut off in mid-sentence.

"Mr. Keane, there's nothing for us to talk about. I don't know how you got my name, but there's nothing I can say to you."

Jack was taken aback. That was a different reaction than what Becky had led him to expect. "I'm confused, John. My assistant said you were willing to talk to me about my brother. What's changed in the last seventy-two hours?"

"Listen, it's not that I'm not empathetic But I didn't realize the call was about a past criminal investigation. It's not my place or privilege to discuss it. I'm sorry, but that's the way it is."

"Well, how am I supposed to find out why you were interested in my brother? Damn it, Lettman, it's important!" Jack was losing it.

"Talk to whoever gave you my name. That's all I can say." He disconnected.

Jack was still at his desk when Ralph came in. He told him about the stiff arm from the former CID Lieutenant. "What could have changed his mind so fast?" Jack asked his military navigator.

"We don't know what we don't know," Ralph repeated Jack's axiom.

As they drove to the Navy Yard later, Ralph suggested they keep the Lettman call to themselves, for now.

"Why?" Jack probed.

"I'm not sure, Jack. I just sense we play it later."

■   ■   ■   ■

Seated in Ed Stanley's office, Ralph and Jack looked on as the JAG major maintained a stoic expression. The two had invested forty-five minutes presenting their case, the set of dots they connected to implicate Eric Walters in murder. "Come on, Ed," Ralph argued, "you have motive and opportunity. Walters is a class A low-life, Keane a straight arrow breathing down his neck, and the SOB found a way to nail our guy."

Stanley sprung to his feet, the chair springs celebrating their sudden liberation with a whooshing sound. "No sale, amigo."

He faced Jack. "This isn't a case anyone is going to indict on," the lawyer continued. "Don't get me wrong. I'm sure Walters is a bad apple. No doubt he ripped off the taxpayers, dishonored the Corps, and probably is guilty of tax fraud. However, that doesn't mean he's guilty of murder. 'Yes' to motive; 'maybe' on intent; but 'no' to any evidence of murder."

Jack knew Stanley was right on the facts, yet wrong on their conclusion. Walters was guilty of murder, either directly or through a surrogate. Either way, he was responsible. He had no doubt. "Okay, so where do we go from here?" Jack asked.

"What about an envelopment instead of the frontal assault?" Stanley suggested.

"So we go after Walters from a different angle?" Ralph asked. "Keep going."

"You've developed an interesting profile of retired Master Sergeant Walters. No mortgage on his penthouse in Jacksonville Beach. No other debt, except a credit card he uses infrequently and pays off immediately. Top tier credit rating. Only visible income besides his retirement pay was from a motel business, yet the guy has acquired a net worth that exceeds $2 million—and that's just the real estate assets he's accumulated. How did he manage to pull that off? I'm no certified financial planner, but how do you parlay a service pension and rinky-dink motel into that type of money with no other visible means of support?"

"So we go after the money trail," Jack said. "But take that to its conclusion. Let's assume we nail him. What's the best outcome?"

"Income tax fraud. No statute of limitations. Disgorgement plus penalties, maybe some jail time."

Jack played it out. "So the best case is Walters gets stripped of some of his assets, with maybe a year in some minimum security situation?"

"That's a fair summation."

"That's not justice. I'm not disputing your analysis, Ed—I just don't like the outcome."

Stanley nodded. "I know. But that's as good as it gets, and even that's not a slam dunk. Getting to yes on tax fraud ain't gonna be a lay up."

■　　■　　■　　■

They were quiet on the drive back to the Tysons office. Jack had the wheel. What Stanley said was logical and not unexpected, but it still left him with a sour taste. Tax fraud would be a long march, with minimal sanction. And the sergeant had already avoided justice for thirty-five years.

"Jack, we're looking at this too narrowly," Ralph injected into their silence.

"How so?" As they approached the I-495 cutoff, Jack focused on navigating into the exit lane to join the traffic heading west.

"If we go after Walters on the money trail, it's liable to stir up other folks, don't you think? He wasn't a lone ranger. Even though they're probably inactive, I gotta believe his brothers would rather keep things dormant."

"So we go after Walters, and assuming some of his network are alive and mentally competent, then what? Where are you heading?" Jack accelerated into the passing lane to get by a tractor-trailer.

"Don't know. I sense we might create some collateral damage for Walters—intentional damage, that is. Maybe we stir the nest a bit, assuming there is a nest, and justice can be facilitated."

Jack looked over at Ralph. *Not a guy I want to go up against*, he thought.

CHAPTER TWENTY-SIX

The meeting was at the Inn at Ponte Vedra. They reserved a private room for the afternoon.

Walters initially resisted a face to face get together but ultimately acquiesced. In their telephone conversation the morning before, the retired Marine suggested to Jack they cover whatever needed discussing over the phone.

"You said you had new information," Walters replied. "Well, what is it? What do we need to get together for?"

"We need to discuss it face to face, Sergeant Walters." Jack continued to keep Walters in his martial box.

"Well, you can suggest all you want, but I don't see what it has to do with me. I've told you everything I can. And I don't like people snooping around my personal business. What gives you the right to run a credit bureau report on me?" His voice had escalated to a shout.

"The right of a next of kin, sergeant, who wants the truth about why his brother died. The right of a brother that now has evidence that a lot more was going on in Materials Company than just filling requisitions." Jack delivered the rebuttal in a firm, steady cadence, not loud but hard.

Walters hesitated. He was about to slam down the phone but recalled the Colonel's admonition about his temper.

"Jack, I don't know what you're talking about. If you have something that makes you question how your brother died, why don't you just fax it to me. Let me take a look, and maybe we can clear this up."

A chink in the defense. "No sale, sergeant. You want to see what I'm talking about, we meet face to face."

"And if I don't?"

Jack expected that gambit. "Have it your way. I just want this resolved. But if you won't invest the time or effort, I'll go to Plan B."

"What's Plan B?"

"I get other folks to help out, folks interested in tax returns, assets, income from offshore sources, that kind of help. Maybe some CID assistance, dusting off some old investigative reports, Operation Shade type stuff. "

"That's bullshit, Keane. You know that. You've got some bug up your ass that I'm involved in your brother's death, and it ain't right!"

Jack purposely waited five seconds before replying. "Prove it."

They finally agreed to meet the following afternoon.

■　　■　　■　　■

Walters was surprised to find two men seated at the table when he entered. Jack noted the raised eyebrows on the oval face, slight jowls, the thin-lipped mouth turned down at the corners. Walters stood five-eleven, 210-220, sixty-five years old, Jack estimated.

"Who's Keane?"

"I am," Jack replied, not rising from his seat or offering his hand. "This is Mr. Gutierrez."

Ralph nodded at Walters.

"I thought we had a meeting between you and me, Keane. What's with the extra baggage?"

"Mr. Gutierrez is assisting me. He's important to our discussion. I invited him."

"How's he important? Are you a lawyer or something?" Walters fixed Ralph with his best glare.

"No, I'm not a lawyer," Ralph answered. "I'm in the military. The Marine Corps."

Walters glared at Jack. "Feels like an ambush. I don't like surprises." He was obviously vexed, shifting his weight from one foot to the other. Jack guessed he'd pivot and head for the door.

"Your choice, sergeant. Either take a seat and we'll get down to business, or leave. Nobody's going to force you to stay."

"Damn right nobody's going to force me." Walters came to a decision and sat across from Jack. He sat on the edge of the chair, weight forward, as if declaring physically he was willing to stay but ready to depart the instant it pleased him. Ralph was to Walters' right. A water carafe and four glasses on a tray centered the table.

"Okay, let's get started," Jack said. "This was in my brother's sea bag." Jack slid a copy of the note across the table. The Gunny caught it, looked at Jack, then read it.

"What was the package you gave my brother, sergeant?"

Walters was silent, obviously surprised. "What was in the package?" Jack repeated.

"It was cash. I made some money on the side, nothing serious, and I needed it sent back to the States. Your brother agreed to take it out of country for me, so it could get mailed home without being inspected."

"How did you make the money? Selling supplies?"

Walters didn't rise to the bait. "No, I made it on slots, playing poker. Gambling winnings. Nothing illegal. I just didn't want to draw attention."

"They paid out slot machine winnings in U.S. dollars?" That came from Ralph.

Walters turned to Ralph. "No, they paid them out in script, Military Payment Certificates. But you could convert MPC to dollars."

"Not through the paymaster's office. Not without raising a lot of red flags."

"Right, hot-shot. Good for you. But the pay office wasn't the only place to convert money. You could do it on the street. That's what I did. And, yes, I know that wasn't allowed. But I did, and it's old news."

"How much money are we talking about, sergeant?" Jack resumed the lead.

"That was 1967, for crying out loud! How much did you make in 1967?" Walters raised his hands in frustration. "A couple of thousand. Small beer."

"What was the team my brother refused to join?"

"The Materials Company team, Jack. Your brother was a loner, a recluse, what we used to call a case. He kept his own company, didn't mingle. I assume that's what he's talking about, but that's just my guess. Only your brother knows, and he can't tell us."

Walters leaned back a notch in his chair, as if signaling he was now in command.

"What was the boys in the band?"

"We already went over that, Jack. I don't know what the hell your brother was talking about."

Neither Jack nor Ralph had anticipated that twist. "Shacked up with some kindred spirit?" Ralph repeated slowly.

Walters knew he had gone a step too far. But it was recoverable. "Suffice it to say that Merrick appeared to have certain inclinations. Nothing that was proven, but everyone suspected he liked being around the guys a little too much."

"What does that have to do with you arguing with my brother, Walters?"

"Only that Merrick seemed to have a thing for your brother, Jack. Now he probably won't admit it. I'm sure he didn't like me riding your brother to get his act together." He hesitated, then continued. "For what it's worth, Jack, I don't believe his interest in your brother was reciprocated."

"You rotten bastard," Jack growled. "So now you're going to claim . . . to suggest . . . " Jack was now the one groping for the right word.

"What *are* you saying?" Ralph asked Walters.

"I'm not saying anything. I'm just trying to help you understand there was a lot going on back then, and I see no value in raking stuff up."

CHAPTER TWENTY-SEVEN

Rock Creek Capital's offices were on 14th Street, between H & I. Jack owed Roland Haskins a face to face debrief on his Hong Kong trip, and he'd deliver it at ten-thirty that morning.

Jack acknowledged his less than total immersion in Quantamica. That was atypical, his norm being total absorption in an assignment—nail the issues, develop the fixes, and implement pronto. In self absolution, he rationalized he was up-front with Roland at the start about his personal situation. And he had inserted a capable shadow executive, adding a lot of value in the U.S. operations.

His unease was more from his failure to uncover the real story in Asia. True, the immediate cash demands which triggered Rock Creek's request for help had dramatically reduced since he got involved. Roland and his partners appreciated the fast, positive impact. But Jack knew big knowledge gaps remained, and he wasn't accustomed to so many loose threads. His instincts flashed *red alert*, though he couldn't finger the precise root cause. *Because I feel it* didn't typically underpin his advice to clients.

Ephraim would drive them into the District. They talked briefly by phone the night before while Jack was en route from Florida.

"What's the situation on your other project, Jack?" Ephraim asked.

"Complicated. Let's update each other on the drive in tomorrow morning. See you at a quarter of ten."

■   ■   ■   ■

Ephraim pulled up in front of Jack's building on Washington Street in an Audi TT. Jack scrunched his large frame into the passenger seat, tossing his briefcase to the back.

Traffic heading up the G.W. Parkway wasn't heavy. The bow wave that flowed from Virginia into the capital each weekday morning had subsided.

"How was the trip back?" Ephraim asked.

"Fine. Got in about nine last night"

"Was the meeting productive?"

"That's not the label I'd put on it, Ephraim. I'd say it was provocative." Jack didn't elaborate, and Ephraim let it be.

"Let's talk about Quantamica's ownership structure," the accountant continued. "First, the U.S. company is privately held, with Rock Creek owning seventy-five per cent. Two other investors hold ten points each, and the management group retained five."

"How about Asia Pacific?"

"Different structure entirely. Rock Creek and the two minority owners have a combined half interest. A Hong Kong registered investor controls the remainder."

"Who's that?" Jack asked as they crossed the 14th Street Bridge.

"A holding company, New Asia Ventures. I have no idea who's behind them," Ephraim added, anticipating the question. "But now that Chung has collected so much, plus your implant's positive impact on the U.S. operations, the demand for cash from the investors is down substantially. Instead of the original ten million request, it's down to three. Roland's a lot happier."

After a moment's silence, Ephraim continued. "What are you going to tell Roland? All is well, steady as she goes?"

"I wish I could. But it's much deeper than slow paying clients and lousy forecasting. I'm going to suggest Roland get private counsel, quickly. The criminal kind."

If the attorney in Ephraim was surprised, he hid it. "Yeah, it did turn around way too fast. What is going on?"

Jack told him what he suspected. Then he repeated it when they met with Haskins. After initially protesting, the investor thought through what Jack told him, then called his lawyer.

■   ■   ■   ■

Ralph's appearance at the JAG office was unexpected. He knew from his own sources that Stanley was in, and alone. After a quick rap on the door, he opened it, catching the lawyer turning back from the window.

"Got a minute, counsel?" Ralph began, but continued into the office, closing the door.

"I guess so," he replied, "as long as it's not for any more free advice."

"No, no more advice. Just some truth. Tell me about your call with John Lettman."

■   ■   ■   ■

"I didn't expect to see you again," Andy started. "Not that I'm complaining. It's nice to have company, especially during the week. Just didn't expect it."

"Andy," Jack started, "thanks for meeting again. I need your help."

Andy waited to hear more, but Jack stopped. Merrick focused on Jack's face, slowly realizing that the buttoned down consultant was fighting to maintain his composure. His eyes were moist, glassy. Jack took deep breaths, wrestling for control. His clenched hands barely rested on the table.

"How can I help, Jack?"

"I need the truth about my brother's death. You can tell me more. We talked to Walters. I have trouble believing him. I don't know the truth. I wasn't there. But you were. I'm asking for your help to get to the truth."

"What did Walters tell you?" Andy asked with no emotion.

"Does it matter? You know Walters better than me. I want to hear it from you. Last time we talked, you left some things out. I don't know why. But I decided the best thing I could do was appeal to you, as someone my brother treated with respect." Jack let silence emphasize his last point.

"I'm asking you to treat him with respect, even though he's dead. I'm asking for the rest of the story, whatever it is. And Andy, I'm not looking for a particular ending, just the truth. Even if the truth is ugly."

"You have a deep faith, right Andy?" Jack continued. Merrick nodded.

"You believe in man's fallen nature? I do. Daniel was human, so he was flawed. I'm looking for the truth, even if that truth includes my brother's flaws."

Ralph watched the two men intently. He felt like an observer behind a one-way mirror. Each man was wholly focused on the other.

"Jack, your brother was one of the least fallen guys I knew." Andy stopped, looking reflective. Considering? Reminiscing? Jack wondered what was swirling in the man's head.

"No doubt Gunny Walters told you some things about me."

"He did. Or at least what he claims."

"That's Walters. Sees everyone else's flaws. And then uses them." Merrick sighed.

"What did Walters use against you, Andy?"

Merrick's eyes searched Jack's, probing for the intent behind the question.

"My . . . inclinations. Walters threatened to have me court-martialed. Said he'd crucify me unless I played along."

"How did he want you to play along? What was he after?"

"He wanted to set your brother up. To shut him up."

"How did he use you to set up Daniel?" Jack probed.

Andy looked up at that corner where the glass met the ceiling again. "Told me to spend time with your brother. Get to know him. Come on to him. Get close."

"Did you?"

"I did spend some time with him, but not the way Walters wanted. Your brother was a nice guy. He could carry on a dialogue, a conversation. And he didn't treat me like a leper." Merrick became reflective again.

"What happened?"

"Walters got pissed off. Said things were coming to a head, and I needed to get off my ass. Finally, he lost it. One night . . . that night . . . he comes by the club, grabs me, and takes me outside. Says I'm to go over to the bunker. What bunker? I ask. I had more than a few pops by then, probably nine, nine-thirty at night.

"The Eagle Scout's bunker, he says, up real close, breathing in my face. He smelled like he had had a few too. And then I'm coming over and threaten the bastard that I'm bringing him up on charges.

"But he's not going to do anything like that, Gunny, I said. That ain't the way things are.

"It don't matter, Merrick, he says, poking me in the chest. I'm going to accuse him, you back me up, and he doesn't have any choice. It's my word against his, and as long as you back me up, I've got him nailed.

"I know I was half wasted, but it still sounded screwy. But that won't work, Gunny. Who's going to believe that? I asked him.

"Nobody has to, Merrick. As long as you and I stick together, Keane's got no choice but to go along to get along. I'll tell him I'll drop it as long as he stops the bullshit, finishes his tour, and gets the hell out of here. Now move! he says and pushes me toward the warehouse bunker."

The visitors waited, mesmerized.

"But just like I figured, it didn't work. Walters goes storming off. I said screw that, I'm not doing it. What's the Gunny going to do, shave my head and send me to Vietnam? So I go back in the club, have another drink."

"That was all on the night Daniel died?" Jack asked.

"Yeah. That night."

Jack and Ralph exchanged a glance pregnant with confirmation. Now they had motive and opportunity. Walters, his resolve fortified with alcohol, took things into his own hands when Merrick didn't come through on the set up.

"Then what happened?" Jack expected Merrick to pick the narrative up the morning after, with Walters' phony request to go find Keane.

Andy looked up. "The next thing I know, Walters is back. He walks me out of the club. I told you to get your ass over there! I been waiting and you're sitting here? Get going, or I'll fix your sorry ass too! And he shoves me again.

"So I got going, all right. And I figured that it was time for the Gunny to get his due. I made a detour through our hut and pulled a frag off my cartridge belt. I had had enough that night—enough to drink, enough of Gunnery Sergeant Walters, enough of being treated like a piece of crap—and I decided it was time to settle some scores."

Jack and Ralph were on an unexpected leg of the journey, mute as Merrick continued.

"I went over to the bunker. Took me a couple of minutes, had to take a leak on the way. I got there, and the Gunny and Daniel are already inside. Damn, I'm thinking. I don't want both of them, I just want that prick Walters alone so I can frag the bastard once and for all. But now that ain't going to work."

Andy paused, recalling that night.

"Daniel, it's me, Merrick, I call from the entrance. Come out for a minute. We need to talk.

"Instead, the Gunny puts his head up. Get your ass in here, Merrick!

"Okay, Guns, you want me in there, I'll come. But you ain't coming out, Gunny, I thought. So I go in. And they're both standing there in the midst of a real situation, you could say. Looked like they had been in each other's faces.

"Tell him! Walters yells at me.

"Tell me what? Daniel asks, looking at me.

"I'm telling you, I says, to get the hell out of here, Keane, as I raised my hand and pulled the pin on the grenade."

Absolute silence accompanied the revelation. Andy Merrick had raised his arms, pantomiming the motion of pulling the pin from the grenade.

LAST EFFECTS

"I wasn't so drunk that I forgot to hold the spoon down. So now I've got a live grenade, the Gunny's up against the back wall, I'm between him and the exit and Daniel is standing off to my left.

"Get going, Daniel, I said. I'll be out in a minute.

"Don't do it, Andy, he says. It ain't worth it. He ain't worth it. Come on, walk out of here with me. Let's stop this, now.

"And he starts walking towards me with his hand out. Hand me the pin, and we'll put it back in. Just keep the spoon depressed. That's it." Andy came out of his hypnotic delivery.

"Jack, your brother was calm. Like he had the situation in hand. No yelling, just quiet confidence, talking to me all the time, holding out his right hand for the pin, ignoring Walters.

"Then the Gunny comes barreling through, heading for the exit. But he knocks into me as he runs past! And I drop the grenade." Merrick looked down at the table top, as if he saw the grenade again, rolling around at his feet.

"I look down, it's there on the ground, and I'm frozen like a deer. I couldn't move."

Merrick looked to his left. "But Daniel was already moving toward me, shoving me back toward the exit with his right hand, grabbing a sandbag, lunging, trying to cover it." Merrick's eyes returned to Jack's.

"And he did. He did cover it. But not enough. The sandbag took a lot of the blast, but your brother took the rest." Silence.

"Finally, I got up. Walked out of the bunker in a daze. No Walters around. I go back in. Daniel's dead."

"No one came running at the sound of the explosion?" Ralph asked quietly.

LAST EFFECTS

Merrick turned to Ralph for the first time, as if only then realizing his presence. "No, we had a 105 millimeter battery right outside the wire. Those guys were firing H&I all the time, harassment and interdiction. Nothing unusual in a blast that time of night. No one came around.

"So I just sat there. I didn't have a mark on me. Didn't know what to do. I'm sobered up by now. Great, I'm thinking. Managed to kill the wrong guy.

"Gunny finally comes back. Looks at me, goes inside, comes back out. Asks me if anyone else has been there? No, I'm answering like a zombie.

"Are you hurt? he asks. No.

"Okay, come on. Get cleaned up. Nothing more we can do here. And he takes me back to his area. Tells me he'll protect me from a murder charge. I just need to keep my trap shut. Just stick to the story. Loner, drugs, depressed.

"And that's what I did."

CHAPTER TWENTY-EIGHT

The retirement ceremony was a small affair, at Ralph's request. Ten guests, including the guest of honor, a private room at the Marine Barracks' mess.

Ralph's commanding officer, Colonel Thomas Brady, presided. Ed Stanley and Stanley's C.O., Colonel Mike Carpenter, were there. Also Master Sergeant Sam Trueblood, Ralph's vision of the Marine from central casting—square jaw, compact fire-plug frame, salt and pepper short cropped hair, and a name that perfectly described the man's character. Two of Ralph's other friends from the Corps. Two colleagues from Headquarters Battalion. And Jack Keane.

Brady's remarks included a narrative of Gutierrez's forty year service history. Jack knew some of it, but the correlation between his résumé and United States foreign policy challenges since the 1960s struck home. Vietnam, Lebanon, the Persian Gulf, Iraq, Afghanistan, the Soviet Union. Then the citations, including two Purple Hearts, the Silver Star, and others that Jack couldn't appreciate the significance of. Brady closed his remarks by reading the retirement order.

Jack shook Ralph's hand in congratulation. "I appreciate everything you've done for Daniel, my father and me. Thanks for taking the time and investing yourself in this. It's had a profound impact."

Ralph smiled. The last eight weeks had affected him too, but he didn't know how to express that in words and so didn't try. He felt at peace with his retirement, closing out those chapters of his life. Somehow that sea bag was a metaphor of unfinished business for him, too—the way it went missing, its arrival as he retired, the misrepresentation of a man's character and death, the unpunished crime of a Marine who abused his position and his men.

"I owe you for bringing me in, Jack. It finished well."

■   ■   ■   ■

The Asia edition of the *Wall Street Journal* picked up the criminal action against Quantamica Asia Pacific, but the story didn't have legs into U. S. coverage. The cooperation between Chinese and United States law enforcement agencies in uncovering and prosecuting the illegal enterprise masquerading as a software and services company was heralded as indicative of the ever stronger ties between the two trading partners. Mr. Alex Chung, until recently the managing director of the Hong Kong firm, had not yet been detained for questioning, but the authorities remained confident he would soon be in custody. The article went on to report that the investigation had been materially assisted by the cooperation of Quantamica Asia Pacific's former United States affiliate, now doing business as Applied Business Insight.

■   ■   ■   ■

LAST EFFECTS

Ralph Gutierrez decided to cross the United Sates by motorcycle, using the trip to reflect and plan. He developed a list of one hundred things he wanted to do, and looked forward to lining through one of them. His itinerary took him through St. Louis, so he'd look in on Abby Whittaker. He might take a short hiatus there, if it felt right.

■   ■   ■   ■

Eric Walters quietly sold his ocean front penthouse in Jacksonville Beach, taking a below market, all cash price. He moved his remaining domestic assets offshore and took the additional precaution of purchasing a second identity. He knew Jack Keane would implement Plan B and sic the IRS and others on him, irrespective of what Andrew Merrick divulged about the truth of Keane's death. But he wasn't overly concerned on that front, knowing he was a small fish in the scheme of things. The plodding nature of the legal system, if things ever got that far, gave him plenty of runway. No, his concern was for his brothers in the band, the small group that had benefited greatly from illegal commerce, lining their pockets with purloined cash. He didn't know how his procurement brothers would respond to the unwelcome attention the case of Corporal Daniel Peter Keane generated, but he wasn't going to hang around to find out. There was too much at stake.

■   ■   ■   ■

It was Tuesday night, so the menu was spaghetti and meatballs. David Keane asked his son to join him in the Birchmere dining room. As Jack entered the building, he said hello to the two nurses seated at their central position with a clear line of sight down both hallways. Trudy, the lead nurse, smiled back and waved. "He's in his room," she volunteered without being asked.

David Keane was listening to *The Pearl Fishers*, which he immediately muted as Jack crossed the threshold. *Door open to the world again,* Jack noted. *Good sign.*

The elder Keane smiled up at his son and started to push himself out of the lone armchair. "Don't get up, Dad. I'll sit on the side of the bed."

"Thanks, Son, I may need a hand up when we go in to dinner." After he resettled himself, his father asked Jack how business was.

"Busy, Dad. Started a new assignment, and it looks interesting. It'll require some travel, but nothing exotic."

"Did you see Major Gutierrez before he left town?" David Keane's tone was casual, but it raised Jack's antennae.

"No, but I talked to him on the phone. He said he was all set to head out."

"He stopped by to say goodbye. Said he appreciated you ignoring his original advice to let things lay. That the Marines always take care of their own, and you reminded him why that was important. He has a lot of respect for you, Jack."

David Keane paused, then added, "And he gave me something." He took a case from his shirt pocket and offered it to Jack. "Open it."

Inside was the Order of the Purple Heart. Jack took in the image of George Washington, the rich purple color, then looked back at his father.

"Ralph said that medal was awarded to him, so it was his to give. He wanted us to have it. He said Daniel earned it."

Their eyes were still shiny as they walked down the hallway to dinner, father holding tight to his son's strong arm.

LAST EFFECTS

CENTENNIAL BOOKS

ORDER FORM

To order additional copies of *Last Effects*, go to our website at *LastEffects.com*, or complete the form below and send it, along with a check or money order for the amount of your purchase plus shipping and sales tax (if applicable) to:

Centennial Books

1591 Chapel Hill Drive

Alexandria, VA 22304

Please send ____ copies of Last Effects at $19.95 each to:

Name: _____

Street Address: _____

City: _____

State: _____ Zip Code: _____

Phone: _____ E-Mail: _____

Please include $4.95 Shipping and Handling for each copy ordered.

Virginia residents, please add 5% Sales Tax ($1.00) per copy ordered.